Lee Bryce has been a top management consultant, coach and trainer for over 20 years. She now works for the Change Partnership in London. She is the author of two previous bestselling business books, *The Influential Woman* and *The Influential Manager*.

The Coach

Lee Bryce

PIATKUS

Visit the Piatkus website!

Piatkus publishes a wide range of bestselling fiction and non-fiction, including books on health, mind, body & spirit, sex, self-help, cookery, biography and the paranormal.

If you want to:
- read descriptions of our popular titles
- buy our books over the internet
- take advantage of our special offers
- enter our monthly competition
- learn more about your favourite Piatkus authors

VISIT OUR WEBSITE AT: www.piatkus.co.uk

Copyright © 2002 by Lee Bryce

First published in 2002 by
Judy Piatkus (Publishers) Ltd
5 Windmill Street, London W1T 2JA
e-mail: info@piatkus.co.uk

The moral right of the author has been asserted

A catalogue record for this book is available from the British Library

ISBN 0-7499-2322-9

This book has been printed on paper manufactured with
respect for the environment using wood from
managed sustainable resources

Typeset by Action Publishing Technology, Gloucester
Printed & bound in Great Britain by
Biddles Ltd, Guildford & King's Lynn
www.biddles.co.uk

Chapter One

It was perhaps fitting that the transformation of Simon Bruce's life began on New Year's Day. He was trudging through mud on the Cotswold Way, walking back towards his country home in Hawksbury Upton, Gloucestershire. His two children, Katy and Edward, were walking with him in companionable silence. Simon was rather preoccupied. His wife Emily had not joined them for the traditional post-brunch walk. Today the usually happy family meal, the first of the year, had been rather strained. Emily was sulking, in a quiet, dignified manner, about the way Simon had danced with a neighbour's young wife at a party the night before. He was accustomed to being in the doghouse. It was a regular feature of his married life, the crimes ranging from minor breaches of etiquette to serious neglect of his long-suffering spouse. But on this occasion he felt slightly hard done by. He had done nothing to encourage Annabel, who had made a drunken beeline for him when the music started, and he found himself part of a rhythmic foreplay that was so public even he was embarrassed. To make matters worse, before he could disentangle himself from Annabel, her husband came over to them, claiming her with the disparaging words, 'Hop it, Jock, I want my wife back.'

Emily had witnessed all this in frozen silence and refused to speak to him, or even make eye contact afterwards. She still had not thawed nearly twelve hours later. Why do the fates always conspire to make me the bad guy? mused Simon as his left boot sank two inches deep into a patch of slimy greenish mud. I'm a perpetual victim in a world where people constantly scheme to get me into trouble, find me disappointing or put me down. Whatever I do, I seem to fall into a trap laid by a malevolent higher force.

Surprising thoughts from a man of Simon's attainments. Born in Kirkconnell, south of Glasgow, to poor tenant farmers, he had gone on to make quite a splash with his life. A bright lad and a good footballer, he'd managed to get himself into St Andrews University when he was seventeen. There he felt completely out of place, until his quick wits taught him how to mix with the toffs who were the fun people at that establishment. They taught him about lifestyle and manners, even down to how to eat a banana, and most importantly of all how to woo Emily.

She was his passport to the world of his dreams. She opened all the right doors for him. His own drive, quick-wittedness and hunger for success did the rest. At forty-five he had fought his way up to become chief executive of the European division of Andecis, a multinational pharmaceutical company. This was a big job for Simon. Although the Andecis global headquarters was in New York, Europe made up by far the largest region for both manufacturing and research sites. Simon had recently masterminded two significant takeovers of smaller drug companies, doubling the size of Andecis. The markets joined in the applause and the company's share price went sky high. But the first year after a merger is never easy. There were problems with integrating the three companies and getting the wonder drugs each had developed to the market. Simon knew that he was skating on thin ice, but at the moment he was still the golden boy of the pharmaceutical world. 'You don't create value without taking calculated risks' was his catchphrase.

I'm a rich man now, his musing continued. I have a wife from a pretty good stable, as she would say of herself. We've stuck together for twenty years, and hopefully we will do till death. Shame she's rather thickened around the middle, and has taken over from my parents in the relentless lifelong task of bringing me up. She's more like a mother to me than a wife – no wonder we've stopped sleeping together. But it's a solid enough relationship. We're a team, raising the children, maintaining our homes and our social lives. I couldn't do any of this without her. So how can I be so totally, absurdly mad as to be having an affair with Grace?

Grace Lee, a Hong Kong Chinese woman, the founder and

owner of a hugely successful perfume business, had been lobbed into his life like an unexploded hand grenade eighteen months ago. He had previously had three brief affairs, but none of them had threatened his way of life, his marriage, his position in the world or his peace of mind until Grace. She must be the most inappropriately named person in the world. In fact I think her parents should be sued under the Trades Descriptions Act, he ruminated, his boots getting heavier and heavier as the sticky mud nearly doubled their size. Grace was easily the most exciting, scary, bad-tempered woman in existence.

She had a real flair for throwing tantrums, hardly the sort of behaviour Emily and her friends would have indulged in. There was no behaviour in fact, however ugly or embarrassing, his mistress would not display to get her own way. Recently, in the first-class compartment on a flight to Prague, she'd punched a hole in *The Times* newspaper Simon was reading, because she felt he was ignoring her. It was true that he didn't give Grace anything like the attention her body and his deserved. But the deals to buy the two new companies, Delster and Zeus, left him with little time or energy for anyone in his personal life. He had neglected his family as well as Grace.

What Simon did not appreciate was that he was as good-looking in his own way as Grace was in hers. Though now on the brink of middle age, he had kept his youthful athletic figure, his straight back and his hair. His most arresting feature was a pair of deep-set brown eyes, which conveyed both a depth of feeling and a strength of character that women could not resist. Cow Eyes, his mother had called him as a child, and he had grown up entirely unaware of his own attractiveness. At first he was bemused by his success with women and could never quite figure it out. Eventually after a string of conquests he just came to accept that he was a lucky man.

I'm a fraud, Simon decided, filled with foreboding as he thought about his flamboyant, increasingly demanding mistress. The world sees me as a respectable family man. If I can't extricate myself from this mess with Grace my reputation will be in shreds. Once the investors get wind of the problems we're experiencing with the two wonder drugs we acquired with the mergers, that honeymoon will end too.

'I can still smell the garlic,' said his son. They were walking through Garlic Hollow, a patch of woodland on the Cotswold Way where wild garlic carpets the floor in the spring. Last year's leaves lying flat on the ground still gave off a familiar whiff.

'Just four or so months to go to this year's crop.' Katy loved the spring, with fresh green leaves, bluebells and wild garlic blooming in the countryside. 'I'll be sitting my A levels then!'

'You'll walk them,' said Simon, and they fell into a conversation about exams and future careers. Although Katy at eighteen knew that she wanted to study psychology at university, she did not yet know what she wanted to do with her life. Edward on the other hand, at only fourteen, was determined to be a City lawyer. Simon loved his two children more than anyone else. They were the only people who loved him unconditionally in return and did not constantly try to make him feel guilty. I hope that I never have to let them down, he thought, his feeling of foreboding growing as they turned a bend in the track and their home came into view.

It was a large eighteenth-century stone house, set in three acres of garden, standing majestically on a hill, with views of what used to be the owner's estate in the flat countryside below. Simon never forgot his feeling of having finally arrived when he first drove up to the property as the new owner on moving day, fifteen years ago. The house was paid for largely with Emily's money, but he had borrowed heavily to enable them to renovate it, and five years ago had finally paid off the mortgage, and bought a second home in London.

Coming towards them, walking his dog, they saw John the gardener. He lived in a cottage at the back of their house and worked not just for them, but for many of their friends in the area. John and Simon had a friendly relationship, often stopping to discuss world and local events. John knew everything that happened in the village and the ones beyond. He kept Simon up to date and entertained with local gossip. Emily seemed to have cooled slightly towards John in the last few months for reasons Simon couldn't fathom. But she still kept him on as their gardener. After all, he could not easily be replaced.

John looked worried as he came towards them. He muttered under his breath, 'Trouble at mill, brace yourself.'

What the hell does he mean? Simon considered pressing

4

him for an explanation but something told him that John would not want to expand on whatever he meant in front of Katy and Edward. Anxious now about what he would find there he quickened his pace towards the house. The children sensed his mood and walked behind him in silence. And then he saw it.

'A helicopter!' shouted Edward. 'Piers must have come to see you!'

Piers was Simon's boss, the global chief executive of Andecis. He'd borrowed a friend's helicopter to visit Simon in Upper Hawksbury once before when a business crisis had blown up while Simon was on holiday. Simon had been carpeted in his own drawing room. A visit from Piers on New Year's day would not make a good start to the year. However this helicopter, parked on the lawn, manicured to perfection by John, had nothing to do with Piers. Simon had seen it a few times before; in fact he had been in it, on trips to Goodwood and to Cowes. His heart began to thud and his hands felt sweaty in his woollen gloves. 'Happy New Year, Mr Bruce,' said the pilot, who was standing by his machine. Simon found he couldn't speak.

Katy had no such problem. 'Why are you standing out here in the cold? Please come into the kitchen and have a cup of tea with us.'

'That's OK, miss, we will be setting off in a few minutes. We have to get back to London before it gets dark.'

At that moment the front door opened and Grace swept across the grass towards them, tearing holes in the lovingly tended turf with her needle-fine heels. The three of them stood close together as if for protection. She looked incongruous in the grey English countryside in her high-heeled leather boots, leather trousers and fur-lined jacket. Simon and his children instinctively huddled together in their green wellies and Barbour jackets and tried not to stare. Grace wore a smug smile on her face and a glint in her eye as if she had just pulled off the deal of a lifetime. 'I'll see you to-morrow night, darling,' she said to Simon, stepping past without acknowledging Katy and Edward.

'Real fur,' growled Katy the environmentalist.

'Dad!' roared Edward, taking only seconds to work out the nature of the relationship between this visitor and Simon. He ran towards his mother who was visible at the French windows overlooking the lawn. Emily was standing with her arms folded, looking stout and grim.

Simon found his voice. 'Take those boots off before you go into the house, Edward.'

I can't believe I just said that, he thought, at the very moment my whole life is about to fall apart!

Grace, seemingly oblivious to the family drama about to unfold as a result of her visit, stepped into the helicopter, and soon its blades were turning, creating a small hurricane on the lawn. Simon and Katy stepped back as it took off. When Simon turned towards his daughter she had a smile on her face, in marked contrast to Edward's stricken expression.

'So that's what John meant by "trouble at mill".' She grinned.

'Katy, you are far too sophisticated for someone your age.' Katy beamed as Simon spoke these words. Simon didn't know whether to be pleased or ashamed. It was obvious his daughter realised what was going on, and obvious too that she had come down on his side. He'd constantly told Emily that the awkwardness between her and Katy was just a phase, but he knew it to be more than that. His daughter's first loyalty was always to him – whether he deserved it or not. At this moment he knew it was misplaced.

'You had better leave me to talk to your mother,' he said as kindly as he could.

Katy ran off to the kitchen entrance. As she removed her muddy wellies she was joined by her brother, tears streaming down his face. He had been packed off to do the same by a cold and angry mother. 'Don't be pathetic,' said Katy. 'It will all work out.' Edward was not to be comforted, though, and they both walked slowly and heavily upstairs, leaving their parents the privacy they needed.

Katy's smile had done more to calm Simon's nerves than half a dozen Prozac, but he stayed rooted to the spot for a long time. He found himself staring at the bronze Japanese cranes on either side of the steps leading up to the walled garden. He had always been fond of these exquisite pieces of Art Nouveau. They stood on spindly bronze legs, and their twisting necks supported graceful heads with beaks pointing up to the grey sky. According to the previous owner of the house the bronze birds had been there for nearly a hundred years.

Finally, he walked towards the French windows, removed his boots and followed Emily into the drawing room. As he did so, he had a vision of his dream castle crumbling away around him, as if made of sand. For the first time in their married life his wife did not tell him off for leaving his boots on the patio. Simon walked over and switched on the table lamp. Emily looked even grimmer up close than she had at a distance. For a time neither of them spoke. Then she said, 'You know why she came here?'

'To be perfectly honest I don't.'

'She told me that you have been having an affair for years, that you are deeply in love and should be together. She said I would have to let you go, as the children and I get in the way of her seeing enough of you. Only she did not put it so politely.'

'I can just imagine.' Simon, to his surprise, was able to summon up some detachment. Now that the moment he had dreaded was happening he felt strangely relieved and calm. Emily is angry and hurt, he thought, but I may be able to rescue the situation. He began to speak slowly and carefully. 'Only some of that is true. It is her view of things and not mine.'

'It's no use pretending,' snapped Emily. 'I've known about your sordid little affair for at least a year. Your jaunts to Goodwood, Cowes and Deauville weren't exactly discreet. The next time you have a fling why don't you go to Blackpool instead, where you won't be spotted by people who know us? And, incidentally, that's how I came to hear about your three previous escapades as well.'

It's obviously not going to be as easy as I thought. Simon just caught himself before saying this out loud.

'Emily, I wouldn't be so offensive as to try to deny it. I said it was partly true and it is. Grace and I have been having an affair – for a year and a half to be exact. Only I don't love her, I don't want to marry her, and I do not want us to part. I very much do not want that.' It hit home as he spoke these words how true they were.

Emily's flushed face wore a disdainful expression. 'I'm afraid I won't be giving you the choice. I will keep this house and buy myself a pied-à-terre in town. You can keep the house in Holland Park. I've had it up to here, Simon. My life can only improve if I'm on my own by choice, and not left here feeling neglected, cheated on and humiliated by your peccadillos. Miss Lee's visit triggered this conversation, but it was going to happen sooner or later anyway. I am at the end of my tether.'

'Emily, I love you. I don't want us to part. Please give me another chance. I'll never see Grace again, and there will be no one else, I promise. Please forgive me . . .'

His voice trailed off as he caught sight of the Christmas card list book lying on the window seat. The leather-bound volume from Smythson contained twenty years worth of names and addresses of people with whom Emily exchanged Christmas cards. Every year, in early January, his wife went through the cards they'd received, and put a firm diagonal line through the entry of anyone so foolish as to have failed to send one that year. No exceptions were made, not even for people with family bereavements. The following year they did not receive a card from the Bruces. Emily was not a forgiving woman. That thought lowered Simon's hopes considerably. However he gave it a second try.

'Please can't you try to forgive and forget?'

'Simon, you should have thought about how important our marriage is to you years ago. Now it's too late. Besides, your mistress has made me an offer I can't refuse.'

'What!'

'Grace Lee came here this afternoon prepared to buy you. She values you at two million pounds and has offered to pay me that sum if I let you go. Frankly I would have accepted half a million. So half an hour ago I sold you to Miss Lee.'

Chapter Two

Brnnnnnnnnnnnnng. The alarm shocked him awake. It was six am and very dark. Simon woke sweating with fear, alone in his house in Holland Park. The alarm clock mercifully ended a nightmare in which Emily, Piers, Grace and a faceless City analyst were pulling him apart, limb from limb. Usually Simon hated being woken by the alarm, but this morning it was a relief. He lay in his big bed under the soft warm quilt and waited for his heart to stop racing. As anxiety over imminent death faded, anxiety over staying alive took over. The divorce battles with Emily, rejection by Edward and the growing crisis at work all flooded into his mind, and it was hard for him to say which was the worse.

The previous week the regulatory authorities in France had thrown out Evereadiness, the wonder drug for short-term memory loss. There were holes in the documentary evidence, and the application did not get through. This meant a delay of eighteen months in bringing the drug to the market, the length of time it would take to get the resubmission assembled. The company had geared itself up to manufacture and market the drug in the hope that the previous week's news would be positive; the financial implications of the delay were significant. Millions of pounds would now be tied up in manufacturing plant and people, all waiting in vain to produce the drug. Evereadiness had been the main reason for buying Delster. Although Delster was a well-established company with a solid record for good products, it was Evereadiness that was meant to propel Andecis into a leading position in the market.

Simon struggled out of his sweaty pyjamas and stepped

into his shower, letting the hot water pound his weary body. He washed his hair with some organic shampoo that Katy had given him for Christmas. That's going to be the best part of the day, he said to himself, as he left the steamy shower cubicle and wrapped himself in a gigantic towel.

While he dried himself, he thought about Zeus. This was a much smaller company, and the only reason for its purchase had been Time Warp, the drug for alleviating jet lag. Simon knew he would have trouble integrating the two companies at the same time, but he decided to take the risk, as the chance of putting two top-selling revolutionary drugs on to the market was too attractive to resist. Piers had cautioned him against biting off more than he could chew, but ended up backing him when Simon showed him the projected profits. Simon knew that Piers would make him a scapegoat if things didn't work out, but he felt that the chances of success were good enough to go ahead with the deal.

It was looking on this cold February morning as if it might not work. Time Warp had hit problems too. The effectiveness of the drug was proving to be much lower than hoped for, as it only worked on ten per cent of a large sample in the clinical trials in Australia. This meant there was a risk that they would not be able to submit Time Warp to the regulators in October as planned, creating yet another expensive delay. Instead of two new blockbusters for the year after the merger, thus proving his expansion plans to be right and wise, Andecis might now have no new drugs at all for this critical first year. He knew as he dusted himself with Johnson's baby powder that the share price would fall further today.

His premonition was right. The further slight downward slide began as the markets opened in Frankfurt and London. The fall was exacerbated by a depressed stock market, but Andecis shares had fallen further than most of their competitors'. Simon reckoned that by May he would have lost £2 million from the value of his holding in Andecis. These shares, his two houses, (now only one), and a few smaller investments including a pig farm in Wales, were his only capital. His wealth was mostly in Andecis shares, and his personal fortunes rose and fell with those of the company.

I have too much to worry about, thought Simon as he opened his wardrobe door and tried to decide whether to

10

wear a suit and tie today. 'I'm too old for the smart casual revolution,' he muttered to himself. 'I can't face decisions on what to wear at six thirty in the morning.' He decided to go for a particularly sober suit, but smartened it up with a glistening new white shirt from Hilditch and Key. 'Now I really look like a dinosaur in my charcoal-grey suit, dark tie and white shirt, and my Church's black lace-up shoes. At least Emily would like to see me dressed like this. She's always thought that male executives should never wear anything else.'

The £2 million that Simon was about to lose from his Andecis shares was the same amount paid by Grace to Emily for his purchase. He ground his teeth as he remembered that humiliating transaction. He had not seen Grace since the day she visited Hawksbury Upton in her helicopter. He had sent her a note calling off both the dinner date and the relationship. The depth of his revulsion for her now matched the intensity of his previous obsession. Grace did not take kindly to being dumped. She began a telephoning campaign, which seemed to combine a desire to force him back to her and to get revenge. Simon found this rather illogical, but then Grace had always been a person who let passion rather than reason drive her decisions.

She phoned his children at school, his mother, his secretary and a few colleagues at work. Edward could not cope, and Emily was furious. His mother stated that she always knew it would come to this. Cherry, his PA, and his colleagues, all of whom had met Grace, found it easy to see the funny side. They were sorry about Simon's marriage, but cheered him on as he stood firm against Grace. The one thing they all took seriously was that they should collude to keep the news from Piers. Cherry was on friendly terms with Carol, Piers's PA in New York, so Carol was easily persuaded to make sure that Grace never got through to Piers, and that any e-mails from her were deleted before Piers had sight of them.

By late January Grace had begun to realise that she had spent £2 million for nothing. She was livid, and kept up the phone calls, but demanded her money back from Emily. Emily, honourable to the last, repaid the sum immediately, and instructed her lawyers to demand the same amount from Simon. Simon fought back with the best and most expensive lawyers this side of the Atlantic, and soon began to haemorrhage money in a most disturbing way.

With these worries on his mind Simon drove through dark, half-empty early-morning streets from Holland Park to his office in Old Burlington Street, Mayfair. These were the corporate head offices of Andecis Europe. Simon spent some time there, in comfort and style, when not visiting the various manufacturing plants and research sites in his considerably increased empire.

Piers was in town. He was based in New York, but spent two or three days in London every two months. Simon had mixed feelings about these visits. He welcomed a chance to discuss his business strategy and operating plans with Piers, but found him unpredictable and volatile, rather like Grace, now he came to think of it. He never knew whether he would get a helpful steer or a bollocking. He had never worked out how to manage Piers.

Simon arrived at the office with just enough time to check his e-mails for any disaster news before the seven thirty board meeting. He deleted three messages from Grace without reading them, but the fourth had the words 'Dire Warning' against the subject so he opened it up. 'If you don't come back to your rightful place by my side,' it said, 'something truly dreadful is going to happen tomorrow. You can save yourself if you call me by lunchtime.'

He was feeling distinctly edgy as he walked with Robert, his human resources director, along the corridor to the boardroom. Robert was tall, lanky and easy-going with abysmal dress sense. He always managed to look like a schoolboy who had suddenly grown out of his clothes, but didn't care. His image was more that of a naive egghead than a director of a multinational company. However underneath that seedy exterior was a sharp brain and considerable business experience. People who wrote him off soon regretted it. He was fiercely loyal to Simon, who very much appreciated his support.

'I hope she's going to kill me,' Simon said to Robert, and meant it.

'Chin up mate, it's probaby just her death rattle.' He and Robert had discussed the Grace problem many times before over pints of beer in the Green Man, the pub around the corner from the office.

12

'I hope you're right.' Simon was visited once more by that sense of foreboding that had preceded the sight of Grace's helicopter on his lawn in Gloucestershire. 'I don't suppose that things can get much worse.'

He was wrong. At the board meeting Piers was on the attack and he was the subject.

'It's not good enough,' bellowed Piers as he warmed to his attack. 'Buying promising companies won't do anything for the bottom line if that's all you do. Just get off your ass and sort out the operating problems. You promised me the new systems would be ready last November.'

Simon interrupted Piers, hoping to defuse his ire. He was starting to sweat, as he always did in these situations. Even on this winter morning he knew that dark wet patches would soon show under his arms if he had to suffer yet another of Piers's rages. 'They would have been ready in time but Doug hit some major problems.'

'No Simon, Doug Allen actually *is* the problem.' Piers came straight back at him, blue eyes piercing a hole through his forehead. 'He'll be late for his own funeral. We wouldn't be having these problems with Time Warp if the new systems for interpreting chemical data were up and running. And why on earth didn't we have our act together with the documents we needed to get approval for Evereadiness?'

'Because of the problems Doug was having with integrating the information technology architecture after the mergers. Without these setbacks we would have been able to collate our evidence in time.' Simon looked back at Piers, displaying courage he did not feel. Piers was angry, but he was in control and, as ever, supremely confident. He sat at the head of the beautiful old mahogany boardroom table and stared menacingly at Simon.

'You should have had a fallback plan in place. Seems to me you've taken your eye off the ball lately. I hear through the grapevine that eight key managers are thinking of leaving. Three are in Information Technology and three are leading research teams. When they go we can kiss goodbye to their teams as well. One is working on Rondina. Sort it, Simon, or you won't have a job very soon.'

Oh no! Simon wanted to throw up. How did he hear that news before me? Rondina was a drug in the pipeline, the Andecis challenge to Viagra. The toxicology results had been good and, so far, so had the results of the clinical trials. Andecis could not afford any losses of key people on that team. It suddenly struck Simon that he had not had any sex at all for over a month. And this was the first time he had thought about it. Maybe I should offer myself to trial the drug, he mused. I'm probably going to need it.

Simon hated these public humiliations. There was silence in the boardroom. Everyone looked down at their papers and the air vibrated with embarrassment. Eventually, though, Simon found his tongue, and tried to react like a grown-up, despite feeling quite the opposite. 'You're right, Piers, it does need sorting out. I'll report back to you in two months' time when you're next in London, and I'll put a plan of action on your desk in a few weeks.'

Simon kissed goodbye mentally to the skiing holiday he was planning with Katy at half term. He hoped she would understand. He would take her with him to New York after her A levels instead; she would love that. His mind drifted away distractedly to Edward, who had not spoken to him since New Year's Day. Simon called him every week, but Edward was never available, and never returned his calls. Emily swore that she was not stirring, and he believed her. Still, it was hard to take.

Carolyn, the marketing director, began to speak. She was making proposals for spending part of the money budgeted for marketing the two delayed drugs on something more urgent. Simon simply could not get his head around it. I'll just agree and get her to deal with it, he decided. He sat back and watched her as she developed her case. Blond, green-eyed and graceful, she was smartly dressed for the board meeting in a soft pale beige woollen suit. I bet she has a great body under all that material, thought Simon, beginning to cheer up at the thought. Everyone else was giving her their full attention. If only he could be so articulate and confident around Piers.

Carolyn had only been with Andecis for a year, but he had developed a great liking and respect for her. She was competent, intelligent, relaxed and often funny, even in board meetings. As he watched she pulled out a ruler and tapped Piers on the fingers to stop him from interrupting while she was at a critical stage of her argument.

'Oh no, not the Carolyn Miller knuckle rapper!' laughed

Piers, rubbing his knuckles. This ruler had caused a great deal of hilarity when she first used it in the boardroom.

'We career women have to find innovative ways of getting ourselves heard,' she said when the laughter died down. She showed no fear of Piers, only respect and even affection. Affection! Simon could appreciate Piers's outstanding business talents, but affection he could not imagine. He wished he could. Carolyn's attitude had lightened the atmosphere in the boardroom. Right now she was diverting Piers from his frustration with Simon and soothing him in her calm, humorous way.

Piers had been instrumental in bringing her into the company. Apparently they had been friends for years, although Simon was not sure what Carolyn meant by the term friend. He had no women friends, only lovers. Carolyn did not behave like a lover towards Piers, so maybe they really were just friends. He obviously trusted her, in a way that he had never trusted Simon.

Thanks to Carolyn's skilful handling of Piers the board meeting ended on a more positive note. Piers said to Simon as they parted, 'Let's have breakfast at the Ritz tomorrow. I don't need to be at the airport until eleven.' Simon agreed, knowing he would have to shake a few people up today and get started on his disaster recovery plan.

First of all he cancelled all his appointments, including a meeting with his divorce lawyer, and spent the day interrogating his direct reports. What he learnt confirmed everything that Piers had alluded to at the board meeting. True, he had known about most of these problems, but now he had to galvanise his team into action. He decided to deal with Doug Allen, the head of IT, himself, and gave him a dose of what he had received from Piers.

'Look here, Doug, you're letting me down big time. I've been your champion for a year now, but all I get from you is delays and excuses. Piers is after my neck, and if he strings me up there'll be nobody to protect you from the mob. They're all baying for your blood out there, especially after the Evereadiness disaster.'

Doug, a short man, sank down lower in his chair until Simon could hardly see him over the top of his desk. He got red in the face and became very defensive, coming out with the same incomprehensible gobbledegook Simon had heard too many times before. Clearly, haranguing Doug wasn't going to achieve very much.

Later Simon ran into Andy Barton, Doug's boss, in the gents. Andy was annoyed with Simon for threatening Doug. 'If you try to make Doug feel personally responsible for the fate of the company he'll become so discouraged that the integration programme will fall completely to bits.'

Simon rounded on Andy, glad that they were alone. 'Well if you think you know how to manage him then why the hell don't you get him to perform!'

Eventually, walking back to their offices, they reached an uneasy truce to allow Andy the time to get Doug to sort out his demoralised department. Thank goodness the share price is so low, Simon thought, otherwise they would all be off.

Afterwards Simon drove over to the research site at Windsor to speak to David Jones, the head of the Rondina team, arriving late after spending forty minutes in a traffic jam on the slip road of the motorway. He tried to keep the edge of frustration out of his voice as he asked David to speed up the work on Rondina in the hope that they might be able to market the drug the following year.

'I'll give it my best shot,' David said, 'but I'll need a lot more resource to make a tighter deadline. However I can guarantee failure unless the IT department gives us better support. If this company could pull up its socks and start to do some planning and organising we might not have so many disasters.'

Simon let this go; even so, he felt stirrings of outrage at being criticised by someone several layers below him in the hierarchy.

It was with a sense of having got started on a journey up a steep slope that Simon drove to the Ritz the next morning. His peace of mind, a fragile thing these days, only lasted for the duration of the fifteen-minute journey. Just as he found a parking place in St James's Square his mobile phone rang. It was Carolyn. 'Have you seen the papers yet?'

'No I haven't. I can't focus until my first coffee.'

'Let me read you the headline from the *Express*. "Simon Bruce rats on wife and mistress." Then it tells the story of how Grace paid £2 million for you, and how Emily returned it when you ran away from Grace. "He did not even have the

16

courage to speak to me and tell me goodbye," Grace is quoted as saying. "Who is Simon's new girlfriend? She must be someone very special to pry him away from these two lovely and wealthy women."'

'I don't need this,' said Simon through gritted teeth. 'This is what she had up her sleeve when she sent me that threatening e-mail yesterday. My only hope is that Piers doesn't read the *Express*.'

'It's in every paper, Simon. It even got a small mention in *The Times*.'

'Thanks for the warning, Carolyn. Just phone a few headhunters and tell them to expect a call, will you?'

'Best of British, sunshine. It can't get any worse. Come and see me after the breakfast.'

'Cheers.'

His heart was in his shoes as he walked down Jermyn Street past Hilditch and Key to the hotel, like a lamb going to the slaughter.

Chapter Three

When Simon walked into the dining room at the Ritz the waiters were as impeccably polite as ever. Maybe they haven't seen the papers yet, he mused. But Piers had. Strewn across the breakfast table, covering his place setting, were seven newspapers. He could see his photograph with Grace at the Mont Blanc hotel in Mégève. The photograph caught them standing in the lobby in their ski suits, with Grace's French movie star friends. It was a good thing the photographer had not taken the picture on the slopes, because Grace was a terrible skier, and spent most of the day having tantrums. Some papers carried a smaller picture of Emily.

'Sit down, Romeo.' Piers was smirking. 'You're not as big a shot as you imagine. You're not on the front page of any of the serious papers, and the *Financial Times* has declined to print the story at all.'

'That's the least of my problems.'

'So this is what's been distracting you from dealing with the problems at Andecis. Who's the new girlfriend? She must be quite something to pull you away from Grace Lee.'

'Would you like some coffee, sir?' asked a dignified elderly waiter, holding a silver coffee pot. Simon thought that waiters had a game they played to keep them from getting too bored, which was to see if they could interrupt their customers' conversations at the most inappropriate moment. This one had succeeded. Simon waited impatiently until the waiter had finished fussing over him before he answered his boss.

'Listen, Piers. I have two things to say to you. One is that the only woman in my life right now is my daughter Katy. The other is that I'm truly sorry to have brought disrepute to the firm like this. Please accept my resignation and resist the temptation to rub my already bruised nose in this shit.'

To Simon's surprise Piers started to laugh. 'I'm not going to allow you to resign. You can't run away and leave us with this mess. The Grace Lee scandal will soon be out of the papers, but you have a year's hard labour to pull Andecis around. I'll be on your back, and I'll support you, but I won't let you off.'

Simon, too stunned to speak, felt the emotion welling up in his throat, and tears prickling at the back of his eyes. Piers looked away to give Simon time to compose himself. He's sympathetic! Simon realised. Wonder and gratitude were novel emotions for him. Everything he'd achieved in his life so far had been through hard grind, fighting against fate, and exploiting his few opportunities to the full. He had built a wall of defence against Piers, which was never high enough, but at least it gave him some protection. And now, instead of Piers's rage, he was receiving his sympathy and support. He had no practice in dealing with either. Simon looked out through the tall windows to the garden behind the hotel, and could see the bare branches of the trees in Green Park in the distance. Out of the corner of his eye he could see the elderly waiter hovering with intent, but this time he declined to interrupt. Probably he could sense the intensity of the feelings at their table.

After a few moments Piers began to speak again. Simon hung on every word. 'You've had a bad year. We all have them. I've had more than a few in my fifty-five years. I know, however, that you've got it in you to pull things round. I've seen you do it before. I know how hungry you are and how much grit that gives you. Your strategy to buy Delster and Zeus was right, but you need to make that strategy deliver. The problem is that you've got problems on too many fronts. You can't sort all of this on your own. You need a mentor. It can't be me because I haven't the time or patience. I've got a global company to run and problems of my own. Get yourself a coach. Carolyn brought one with her from her previous company. Ask her if she can put you on to somebody. Actually, let me make that stronger. I order you to get a coach, not because you're a remedial case, but because you're too good to lose, and the stakes are high.'

'You want me to get a shrink?' Simon was bemused and slightly offended. Then on reflection he suspected that he needed one.

'No, not a shrink, a business coach, an external mentor. Someone who can act as a sounding board without breaking your head open as I would do.'

'And you say Carolyn has one?'

'Yes. In fact each member of my top team in New York does too. It's endemic over there. I've even got one myself, but I only see him about four times a year because of my ridiculous schedule.'

'Well, I'll get one if you say I should, but I can't see the point right now.' Simon was too old-fashioned to admit that he found the idea of regular support rather welcome.

'You will.'

Simon tucked into his scrambled eggs and smoked salmon, which he suddenly felt like eating. Support and encouragement from Piers. This was a new experience. Then his thoughts turned negative again. The man has such terrible mood swings. The next big setback and he'll have me out like he threatened to yesterday.

'You've got to make this work, Simon. I don't have much patience as you know, and neither does the stock market.' This was Piers's parting remark as he got into his limousine to go to the airport.

Simon went straight to Carolyn's office when he returned from the Ritz. 'I'm still employed! Temporarily, I suspect, but I'm still here.'

'I knew Piers would come up trumps. He does have a heart under that iron-fisted exterior. Anyway, that's good news. Grace has done her worst, and you've survived. With luck she'll give up now.'

'By the way, Carolyn. Did you soften Piers up before our breakfast meeting? He was as gentle as a pussy cat and even suggested that I get myself a coach.'

'I did speak to him before I called you, and I'm glad it helped. I think you've had as much as you can take right now.'

'Can you help me find a coach? I wouldn't know where to begin, or how to judge if they'd be any good.'

'Come along with me next week to the Institute of

Directors. Robert and I are going to hear Angela Jones talking about transforming yourself. She works for the same organisation as my coach, and has made quite a name for herself with a rather revolutionary book on leadership. If she impresses you maybe she could be your coach.'

'OK. Let Cherry know the details and I'll be there. I think I'm in London next week.'

'Fine. Here's the leaflet. The talk is entitled "The Terrible Twins of Leadership, Fear and Control".'

'I've got fear all right, but I'm totally out of control.'

'Well, that might not be a bad starting point.'

In the lecture room at the Institute of Directors the following Friday he found a fairly select crowd of senior people from a range of industries, and a few people he recognised or knew. Trevor Peters, who ran the Private Wealth department at Morland Stamp, the prestigious investment bank, came over to him.

'Hi, Trevor. What brings you here?'

'Angela is my coach,' said Trevor, 'has been for years. I think she's brilliant. I've brought along a couple of people who need to hear what she has to say.'

'I guess that's how I come to be here. Carolyn thinks I could do with a dose of whatever she has to offer.'

'Are you looking for a Grace Lee recovery programme?'

'Now now, that was below the belt. Is Angela here yet? I want to see what she looks like.'

Trevor pointed out a slim, tall woman, dressed immaculately in an Armani suit.

'That could never be her! I expected someone fat and mumsy, with flowing robes and dangly earrings.'

'I think you're in for a few surprises. She's straight down the middle, a successful businesswoman, company director, married and mother of four. Some of her ideas are alternative but take it from me, Simon, they work.'

Simon went to sit in the front row beside Carolyn and Robert. 'I want to get a good look at this woman. The chemistry has got to work if she's going to become such an important part of my life.'

'How like a man to base chemistry on looks,' Carolyn couldn't resist saying.

But Simon was not basing his scrutiny on superficial

appearances. He liked Angela's poise, her warm, unaffected smile and her purposeful movements. He also liked her long shapely legs, and decided that she was attractive, but not distractingly so. So far so good, he thought. Let's see what she has to say.

Angela Jones stood at the front of the room and began her talk.

'Would you like to live in a reality where you achieve success for yourselves and your companies without engaging in headlong combat, without hard labour, sweat and grind? Would you like your life to be free from fear and struggle, unhurried and free from pressure? Would you like to be full of high energy and enthusiasm, inner peace and harmony? Do you want to regularly experience spontaneous humour and delight, loving friendships and intimate relationships? Hands up if anyone enjoys all of these right now?' No one moved. 'Half of them?' Simon, like the others, kept his hands firmly on the arms of his chair.

'OK, so you probably enjoy a few of these benefits, but less than half. You are a normal audience of senior executives. You probably think that the full package is incompatible with your roles in modern corporate life. Wrong. It most certainly is achievable. But you have to revise your beliefs. Change your beliefs and you transform your world. Why do I say that?

'First of all I'll explain how we shape our external world through our inner world. We know from modern physics that the universe is nothing other than a vast field of energy in which all matter is interconnected, responsive and constantly changing. From Eastern thought and new-age religious ideas we know that we have access to the vast field of energy in the universe. We can project it outward with our thoughts and intentions and influence the reality around us. Heisenberg, Pauli and Bohr, the fathers of quantum mechanics, give further credibility to this Eastern viewpoint.'

Simon's thoughts began to wander. Angela's remarks about modern physics took him back to the first time he met Emily in the chemistry laboratory at St Andrews. She was working over a Bunsen burner looking delightfully pretty in a pale blue jumper and skirt. She wore a string of pearls, and looked completely out of place in the untidy lab.

'I find this all such a bore,' she had said in her posh cut-glass accent. 'Could you help me with it?'

22

'I will if you'll come out with me tonight,' Simon had replied in his broad Scottish tones.

Emily had looked him up and down, 'Give me a hand with this and I just might consider it.'

With Simon's help she got top marks, and they began a long relationship in which he led on science and she called the shots on everything else.

I've always been led by the nose by women, he thought. Could it be that they're only figments of my imagination that I've created?'

Angela's pleasant, enthusiastic voice captured his attention once more; he left his daydreams and rejoined her lecture.

'In a seemingly magical way, our inner thoughts and intentions are what shape the outer world of our experience. Everything in the world is simply one form or another of energy. When we want something, we project our own individual energy by focusing our attention in the desired direction. Where attention goes, energy flows. When we do this we influence other energy systems and attract towards us those people and events that will fulfil our expectations and reinforce our beliefs. We each write our own play, which may be dramatic, boring, loving, hateful, happy, miserable, achieving or unsuccessful. We then act as magnets for people who will fit into our scripts.

'Until people become aware that they create their own reality they are victims of their own plays. This is why I am seeking to make you conscious of the process. If we see a world that we dislike – full of incompetence, danger, greed, power plays, deviousness – we are first of all gazing at what is inside us, at what we believe. The world is a mirror which reflects our inner selves. Our beliefs about the world attract experiences that confirm these beliefs. The more intense the belief, the more magnetically we attract the corresponding experiences. So if you think that the world is a dangerous place, full of people out to get you, that's how your world will be.'

Simon, listening intently to this, had a gloomy insight: so the delays to the drug projects, Piers on the warpath, Grace Lee and my divorce, Edward's rejection of me, all are people and events that I've pulled into my life. What a responsibility!

Angela continued, almost as if she were reading Simon's thoughts. 'Take responsibility for the thoughts and emotions you send out, because they go out into the world and create the events that come back to you. Our minds do not stop within our skulls, but are connected by waves of energy to everything else in the universe, including other minds. Our fear and negativity touch everyone, but so do our love and concern. We do not need to keep living in the unhappy or frustrating plays we've written. We have 90,000 thoughts in a day, most of them negative. Think of the power of turning most of those thoughts into positive ones. Think of the world, the experiences you could create, the joy you could share.'

'That's a very hopeful message, Angela,' said a woman in the audience, 'but it doesn't sound all that easy.'

'What's the alternative?' asked Angela. 'To continue to live in a world that we see as alien and dangerous? To live in fear of the capricious whim of fate, and to use all our precious energy fighting against and trying to control the very reality that we created with our negative beliefs? That sounds even harder to me, and much less pleasurable.'

How does she know so much about me? pondered Simon.

'It's not so hard to trust in the universe. You created it. You are connected to, supported by and able to influence with your thoughts, the other beings you share it with. The universe is benign. It loves you. Put love into it and you'll get it back tenfold. Every religion teaches us this. If you have religious beliefs you may like to think of the universe as God. But this is a caring and loving God of whom I speak, not the harsh, punishing, demanding God of some religious sects. If you believe in a harsh reality you'll create a harsh God. To me, because I believe in a benign universe and a loving God, they are one and the same, and I flip between one and the other in my thoughts. However for those members of the audience who have no religious beliefs, I'll stick to my original terminology and speak of the universe.'

At that point the doors of the lecture room opened and two waitresses brought cups of tea and cakes. It was five thirty on a Friday afternoon, and Simon was both hungry and tired, so he gladly joined forces with the others as they filled up with tannin and carbohydrates.

'Tell me, Simon.' It was Trevor Peters again. 'What are the chances of Andecis getting any drugs to the market this year? I hear you've hit a number of snags.' Trevor sounded sympathetic but Simon couldn't be open with him. Any titbits of unfavourable gossip would be reported to the analysts in Trevor's Private Wealth department within hours. This would not help the sagging share price.

'One hundred per cent certain,' Simon answered. 'It's true we've hit a snag with one, but we're on course with another blockbuster.' Trevor was just about to probe further when Angela announced the end of the tea break.

Simon's thoughts turned away from blockbuster drugs to his religious beliefs as he sat down. Before Angela had a chance to proceed with her talk he spoke up.

'My God, who I inherited from my mother, is the harshest and most unforgiving of Presbyterians. I think for now that I'd rather focus on the power of the universe than on His power, which I've never seen as benign.'

'Feel free to do that,' said Angela. 'Since your beliefs create your reality, if you love the world you'll find continued support, often in unexpected places. Those who believe in a hostile universe live in fear and want to try to control all aspects of their lives, particularly their relationships. This is why I've called this talk "The terrible twins of leadership, fear and control".

'If you trust in the universe, you can let go of your fear and of your need to control, fight and overwork. Turn your intentions, beliefs and visions of the future into happy, positive ones for yourself and for others. You'll see what the universe gives back to you. Once you lose your fear and your need to control, you can flow with life rather that fight it. This is how you achieve success with inner peace rather than turmoil. The Roman philosopher Epictetus told us: "Seek not that events happen as you wish them to happen, but wish them to happen as they happen, and you will go on well."'

That seems like a bit of a tall order for me right now, thought Simon, but he kept his mind open.

'When we find ourselves in seemingly impossible situations, with Augean stables to clean, we're forced to rely on our souls, and on all the other souls in the universe, to whom of course we're connected. To be more scientific about it, we're forced to abandon foolish thoughts of cracking the problem on our own, as an isolated being. Instead we have to seek help from that universal energy, those interconnections with other parts of our benign and supportive universe. God doesn't sit back and laugh at you, saying, "You got yourself into this mess by creating it, now get yourself out." When you enlist his help, the help of the universe and all its connections, you move from fear to trust. You become a channel for higher powers in addition to your own individual strengths, to help you create a solution. You attract into your life the people, ideas and circumstances you need to take you forward over the hurdle. You have no alternative, unless you want to live in anxiety, fear and hopelessness.

'This is the way that nature works, so go along with it and let it work for you, but there is one important condition . . .'

It was beginning to sound so plausible. I hope she's not coming up with a catch, Simon thought anxiously.

'That condition is that your intentions and desires must be ethical, and for the good of others, not just for yourself. As the Dalai Lama says: "If you seek enlightenment for yourself, simply to enhance yourself and your position, you miss the purpose. If you seek enlightenment for yourself in order to serve others, you are with purpose."'

Maybe that's what's wrong with my life, thought Simon. My mission has been to climb to the top, to make money, to keep it and to have fun. The Dalai Lama would not see that as serving. The having fun bit has been at Emily's expense, and it's brought me anything but peace.

'Purpose is why you're here on earth. Once you've found your purpose, your mission, and are acting it out, the universe swings into motion to support you and that purpose. As we've seen, you're in a relationship with all other living things, and you are purposeful and peaceful when you serve in some capacity. The more you choose to be of service, the more profoundly you experience the support of the universe, and the more good things, including solutions to problems, you attract into your life.

'Knowing and living your mission enhances the frequency of meaningful coincidences as you are guided towards your destiny. Carl Jung called this synchronicity. Dreams, intuitive insights, chance meetings, unexpected opportunities, inspirational books, lectures, all lead us in the direction we're destined to go. First these coincidences make our path clear, then they guide us forward and support us as we overcome obstacles.

'Everyone has a mission and purpose in life, and when you

26

find it, you find happiness. To find your purpose ask what makes you unique and different, what activities give you immense pleasure and satisfaction. In these activities lie the clues to your soul's purpose. When we work solely for money, or our own power and status, we miss out on the chance to find that mission. Instead of asking what can I get, and how can I protect it, ask what can I give? Then the universe will give you what you need so that you can give to others.

'There are two parallel universes: one of fear and control, the other of trust, peace and service to others. It's for you to choose which one, as a leader, you will live in.'

As the lecture came to an end Simon sat deep in thought, and hardly heard the lively question and answer session which followed. Angela's points were not entirely new to him, but it was the first time he had considered them in the context of leadership, and of his own particular bag of troubles.

'I suppose this is how synchronicity works,' he said to Angela over drinks and canapés afterwards. 'Fate, which I dare say I created, dumped me in a bit of a mess; colleagues bring me here to hear you talk, and you open my eyes to a way out, to a way of creating a different reality. I would like to ask you to work with me as my coach.'

Angela smiled her sweet, warm smile. 'You seem to have got the basic hang of it. Yes, I'd like to work with you. I'm sure there'll be a lot we can teach each other.'

'You'll be hearing from me,' said Simon, and he left to collect Katy from the station. She was coming to London for half term to do some resting and shopping, as an alternative to the abandoned skiing holiday. Simon's step was a little lighter as he walked round to his car in Waterloo Place.

27

Chapter Four

Katy's half term started off splendidly. Simon took her to see *La Bohème* as an introduction to the opera and she loved it. She was enraptured by the opera house at Covent Garden, the restaurant overlooking the bar, the champagne and the fact that Simon seemed to know half the people in the audience. 'Don't get too carried away,' warned Simon afterwards as Katy sang the wonderful love song from the first act at the top of her voice in the taxi. 'This could become a very expensive addiction.'

They slept very late the next day, then went to see an Art Nouveau exhibition at the Victoria and Albert museum.

'Look, Daddy, there are some things by Jonathon Knox!' Katy exclaimed, pausing in front of some lovely vases. 'Don't you have a mirror by him in your hall?'

'Not so loud, Katy, we don't want the criminal fraternity knowing what valuables I have in my house.'

'I can't imagine there'll be a lot of crooks wandering around the V and A,' Katy laughed.

They then did some desultory shopping at Harvey Nicks and in the early evening had a drink in the bar on the top floor. Here they amused themselves watching the attempted pick-ups, making bets about who would end up with whom.

The next day they had Sunday lunch at the Belvedere in Holland Park followed by a cosy late afternoon and evening spent by the fire as it poured with rain outside. This is the first happy weekend I've had since New Year's Day, thought Simon as he began to read his paperwork in preparation for Monday.

*

He hardly saw Katy after that. His days were long and tiring. He got home before ten on only one evening, which was Wednesday. They spent an hour together in the steam room, sauna and splash pool complex which Simon had installed in the basement two years previously. It had taken nine months to build, and then a further frustrating year to dig up and re-lay the tiles in a way that stopped the water leaking out of the splash pool and flooding the basement floor. Finally he got it sealed tight and working perfectly. Emily had refused to have anything to do with it. She thought the whole scheme was a dreadful waste of money, and in dubious taste. Simon loved it, probably in defiance of Emily, calling it his blue heaven, with its pale blue tiles and off-white trim.

Katy was enjoying herself. She had a number of friends in London and was not short of company. Simon spent the week travelling to research sites, which were all mercifully in the southern half of the country, apart from the Zeus labora-tories in Sheffield. He attended meeting after meeting of top managers around the country. He berated some teams, encouraged others, and got as involved as his rusty scientific knowledge permitted in the nitty-gritty planning to recover from recent setbacks. The process was exhausting, and, he suspected, only partially successful. He felt even more tired as he contemplated the travelling he would have to face to do the same in the other European countries.

David Jones, the head of the Rondina team, tendered his resignation, as the board had feared he might. On the Friday evening he and Simon had a tense meeting over dinner in the Waterside Inn at Bray.

'I only get a sense of panic and urgency, not of clear dir-ection and planning,' he said. 'And I see no sign of the IT crowd getting their act together. If they were doing what they promised we'd be linked in with other teams worldwide and exploiting the advantages of a large global company. As it is I don't see how I can meet those deadlines I committed to at our last meeting unless they produce the infrastructure we need by tomorrow and that isn't going to happen.

'We should all be integrated by now, with instant access to data worldwide. We still waste so much time flying around to meetings, waiting for people to return phone calls, unable to work when systems have crashed. We're literally adding months on to our project by not being where we should be with our IT and having to rely on old technology.' David's prematurely bald head glistened as it reflected the lights in the restaurant. Simon had a sudden urge to take his pen out of his jacket pocket and write 'Doubtful David' on the shiniest part, but thought better of it.

'Everything you say is true, David,' said Simon. 'The IT department has been given six months to sort itself out, and to start hitting deadlines. Why don't you give us the same time to help you to hit your targets? We don't want to lose a good person like you when a solution is around the corner.'

Eventually David reluctantly agreed to Simon's request. But when they shook hands and said goodbye he looked grumpy and unconvinced. Perhaps I should write 'Disgruntled David' on his forehead instead, thought Simon.

At this meeting and at several more Simon learnt of a number of other concerns and gripes that were demotivating the managers and aspiring younger staff. His spirits sank lower and lower as he reviewed the events of the week in his hotel room after dinner. There was open conflict caused by the differences in culture between Andecis and Delster. Andecis had always thrived on an entrepreneurial ethos. They called themselves a ready, fire, aim company and prided themselves on quick decision-making. They gave heavy support to entrepreneurial activity in local environments.

In contrast, Delster was a more solid, mature company with centralised procedures and planning processes. It was important to get agreement from interested parties before action, which made decision-making slow and cumbersome in the eyes of the Andecis managers. To make matters worse, many of the top jobs in the newly merged company had gone to directors from Delster. So Andecis people, accustomed to freedom and speed, were feeling reined in and disempowered.

Simon switched on the television to watch the news, but found he couldn't concentrate. Into his mind flooded a scene he had witnessed earlier in the week. Peter, the financial director, an ex-Delster executive, was emerging from a meeting room with Alan, one of the senior marketing managers. They were both looking very tense.

'If we don't move on these proposals within the next two months we'll have lost the head start we'd hoped to get on the competition,' Alan said, in a voice that sounded like a low growl.

'I do see your point,' said Peter. 'But we can't ignore procedure in this case. There's too much money at stake, and some of the European countries may not want to commit such a big budget.'

'You know the only way Andecis got big was to react with the speed of lightning—' He stopped the conversation as soon as he noticed Simon.

'How are things, guys?' asked Simon.

'Fine, just fine,' answered Peter with a forced smile on his face.

Simon left it at that because he was rushing off to a meeting of his own, but the argument was typical of many he had heard recently, and it registered. He knew that the Delster procedural approach was right for a company as large as Andecis had become. But he worried that they were throwing the baby out with the bath water, at the expense of their competitive edge.

Simon sighed as he unzipped his overnight bag. We do seem to be in a bit of a mess, he thought, removing his clothes and putting on his pyjamas. He went into the bathroom and brushed his teeth with Katy's organic toothpaste. It was not a pleasant experience. He spat out the foul-tasting foam then gargled furiously with mouthwash.

Roger, the human resources director, had warned Simon to expect problems of culture clash if the merger went through, and to consider whether it might fail as a consequence. Simon brushed these worries aside, confident that they would find a way of solving everything. 'After all,' he said to Roger. 'You know what I believe; you don't create value without taking calculated risks.' He struck a deal with Roger not to raise these concerns with Piers, who might at that point have had cold feet about the merger. Instead Simon promised to give Roger a budget to do some culture integration work after the merger. All the integration budget had so far been allocated to that black hole called the IT department.

Simon began to wonder if it wasn't now time to allow Roger to get started on his schemes. Morale did really seem to be low. The people from Zeus were the most disheartened of all. Because their company was very much smaller than the other two, it got no places at the top table. Their senior people felt relegated to middle management and did not like it.

Simon shivered, feeling cold in the hotel bedroom. He then noticed that one of the windows had been left slightly open, and a cold draught was blowing down his back. 'I wish they wouldn't hire fresh-air enthusiasts in these places,' he muttered to himself as he reached up and banged the window shut. He plugged in his laptop and turned it on, opening up his e-mails. After he had counted thirty new messages he shut it right down again, deciding he was too tired, and that early morning would be the best time to tackle them.

Simon got into the big comfortable bed and turned off the lights. He was staying overnight at the Waterside because he had a breakfast meeting with Tony Albertino, his counterpart in the USA, on Saturday morning.

As he drifted off to sleep he couldn't help thinking about yet another problem. At director level there was agony of a different sort, which Simon himself felt acutely. Suddenly they were managing an organisation which had doubled in size. Everyone was stretched to the limit, involved in far too much detail, not delegating adequately and not finding the time to support and develop his or her direct reports.

He rose early the next morning after an unexpectedly good sleep, and dealt speedily with his e-mails before wandering down to meet Tony in the dining room. He chose an un-characteristically healthy breakfast of fruit and cereal. He had endured enough stress lately to play havoc with his digestion without adding cholesterol-laden fried eggs and bacon.

Tony suffered no such inhibitions about rich food, and tucked into a huge English breakfast which there was clearly room for in his expanding paunch. Between mouthfuls he launched into a tale of woe. Simon did not know whether to be pleased or sorry to hear that they were suffering similar problems on the other side of the Atlantic. Piers was around much more in New York than he was in London, of course, which had advantages and disadvantages for Tony. Simon wasn't sure which was worse, suffering terse e-mails and tele-phone calls at odd hours, or being harangued as Tony regularly was by Piers on the golf course and at ridiculously early breakfasts.

Tony was not a favourite with Simon. He had a reputation, which he lived up to consistently, for being Piers's lapdog. He allowed Piers to make all of his decisions for him, obeyed orders assiduously, and gave no indication of being able to use his initiative. Despite this he managed to annoy Piers with great regularity, as he was unable to anticipate his boss's sudden changes of mind. When under attack from Piers he sweated even more profusely than Simon: great beads of the stuff could be seen forming on his forehead, and then trickling down his face. Normally, Simon and Tony had a courteous but distant and formal relationship. This was the first time that Tony had opened up to him, and Simon responded with good-hearted empathy.

'I know what it feels like, mate,' he said to Tony. 'Piers terrorises me in person every two months, and probably once a week over the air waves. You've got a much heavier dose!'

Simon returned home to find chaos. The house looked like a tornado had swept through it; Katy was in tears. There was broken glass everywhere, wine spilled all over the Persian rugs, and the dreadful smell of vomit filled the air. Simon blew his top before Katy had a chance to explain, but when he calmed down enough to listen he felt rather sorry for her, although he also felt very sorry for himself.

With his permission, she had held a dinner party for ten on Friday night. The damage was caused by a group of about fifteen crashers, who forced their way in, ruining her dinner party and his house. When the inevitable fighting broke out they spilled into the communal gardens at the back of the house. There they made so much noise that the neighbours called the police and that belatedly rescued the situation. Katy and Simon spent a sad weary day cleaning up as best they could. When they parted at Paddington Station the next day it was two dispirited and guilty people saying goodbye.

Simon sat in his sauna on his own on Sunday night and thought about the points Angela Jones had made at the Institute of Directors. 'We create our own reality.' Well, I'm making a pretty poor job of that at present. I'll have to ask Angela for a few script rewriting tips. Simon was due to have his first coaching session on Monday. He summarised the basics of her blueprint for a peaceful existence: 'Find your mission in life, inspire with your vision of the future, let go of control so you can let go of your fear, and go with the flow of fate which will take you towards your dreams.'

At this point he became aware of his pounding heart so he got out of the sauna and immersed himself gingerly in the ice-cold splash pool. Returning to the sauna he felt blissfully relaxed for a few minutes as his body heated up again, so he continued with his thoughts about Angela's presentation.

First of all, I am so busy surviving that that is the only mission I can think of right now. If I let go of control my fear would increase as my prospects of earning a living decreased. Go with the flow. I seem to be doing that but only because the flow is so powerful that I can't fight it. I think I have some lessons to learn. My life certainly needs to change. I've lost my wife, my son, given up my mistress, and I have no social life apart from business dinners. I work all hours, have a huge uphill struggle to put the company right and save my job, and have miserable lonely weekends. Angela, you don't know what you are about to take on.

'I think I do know what I am taking on,' said Angela at their meeting the next day as Simon, giving her the background events of his life, reiterated these points. The coaching meeting took place in Angela's office in St James's. It was a pleasant light room with paintings and framed family photographs all over the walls. A large vase of flowers sat on the window ledge. The effect created was of a peaceful homely office, and Simon began to feel relaxed as soon as he sat down.

'I know that things are going badly for you right now,' Angela continued, 'but you have a tremendous amount of ability and experience, combined with a quick brain and an open mind. I think it'll be just fine. I know right now you're thinking that it's all up to you to get yourself out of this mess, and it might just be too much, even for a fighter like you. But I think you're forgetting that you're not on your own. Remember the points I made about the connections you have to all other living things in the universe at a thought level?'

'Yes, that did stick in my mind.'

'When you start to have positive visions of the successes and pleasures you want in your business and personal life, all sorts of forces and coincidences will help you along the way. But you really have to believe that you deserve them and can achieve them. This is how nature works. Before you get started on that I think we'll have to get you to a petrol station and fill you up with fuel.'

'What do you mean?'

'It seems from what you've told me that your life is pretty dreary. It contains no pleasure, no fun and little love and affection apart from what you get from Katy. It provides you with no friendship or support – in other words none of the fuel or spark that would recharge your batteries. If you could wave a magic wand, what things would you like to have back in your life to make it more worth living?'

'Edward, for a start.' Simon's voice caught in his throat as he said that. He had bottled up a lot of emotion over Edward's withdrawal from his life; now, with a sympathetic listener in front of him, he felt it welling up.

'I can imagine how distressing it is for you. I don't think I could cope if one of my children rejected me. OK, let's work on that. You say he doesn't return your calls, just refuses to speak to you. Is there anyone who has enough influence over him to persuade him to give you a short hearing?'

'Only Emily.'

'Do you think you could get her to help? Could you get her to see how damaging it is for a child of Edward's age not to have a relationship with his father? Adolescence is the time when a boy starts to separate psychologically from his parents, particularly from his mother. He very much needs a father around to enable this to happen. It can damage his prospect of being a healthy adult to have you out of his life. I get the impression that Emily is a fair and sensible person, so she might use her influence with Edward if you asked.'

'I'll give it a try, it might work. I need it as much for my sake as for his.' Simon thought for a moment. 'Next I'd like a better work–life balance, a return to some sort of social life, and to have a bit of fun.'

'What can you do about that?'

'Well, Emily always used to say about social life and friend-ships that you reap what you sow. The trouble is she was my social secretary and did all the sowing. I just turned up and had fun, and of course a few affairs, for which I am now infamous.'

'Is there any way you can do some sowing yourself?'

'You're making me do all the work, aren't you?'

'We might as well start as we mean to carry on.' Angela

grinned. 'I'm sure that a hot-shot executive like you can issue a few invitations.'

'I could have a party – a sort of middle-aged coming-out party, debutante style, to announce that I'm back on the social scene. But I don't have the time or energy to do all the work involved in entertaining.'

'There are professional caterers and organisers who'll do all the work for you. I'm sure Katy would love to help too.'

'OK, you're right. Where there's a will there's a way. And, if I start picturing myself with a good social life and work–life balance, people and events will come along to help me get them.'

'You got it right first time.'

'You know, Angela, I need one or two good friends and confidants in my life. You're great. Even from our first meeting I see how nice it is to have someone to talk to who won't judge me or punish me. I'm really looking forward to working closely with you. But now I've got a taste for this I think I'd like one or two other similar relationships. Carolyn and Roger are both sympatico; maybe I could get to know them a bit better.'

'That would be really good. You need all the support, emotional support, I mean, that you can get right now. Remember you work with them, though. Complete openness, like you can enjoy with me, may not always be appropriate with colleagues.'

'OK, I'll watch how I go.'

'You've got a lot to be getting on with. Next time we can begin to explore your mission in life. Don't worry if you can't see it right away, it'll come to you.'

'I guess I'll just have to ask the universe to help me to find it.'

'That will help more than you realise. See you in a couple of weeks.' Angela rose, long-legged and elegant in her floppy trouser suit. She escorted him to the lifts, and smiled a last sweet smile. 'Take care,' she added as he bundled himself into his overcoat and warmly shook her hand.

Angela went back to her office to write up her notes on Simon's coaching session. 'Wow, what an attractive man!' Angela spoke out loud to herself as she searched for her document folder on the computer.

'Surely you haven't let a client turn your head?' Angela had been overheard by her colleague Chris as he walked past her office door.

'Don't worry, it's rather like admiring a Pre-Raphaelite painting. Besides, I'm a happily married woman.'

'Well, you know the rules, look but don't touch.'

'Absolutely.' Angela began to laugh, thinking of how shocked Simon would be if his coach suddenly made a lunge at him. 'All relationships are sexual, Freud taught us that, but it gets a bit naughty if you try to make them carnal.'

'I see you don't need any ethical counselling,' said Chris as he strolled away, putting an end to their banter.

When Angela was alone again she resumed the task of making notes on the meeting with Simon. 'I've seen people with half Simon's problems crack under the pressure,' she typed into the computer. 'But something tells me he has the strength to pull through. He's a brave fighting Scotsman, hardly surprising with a surname like Bruce. Once he gets the hang of going with the universe instead of fighting it he'll be away.'

Simon hit the decks running when he got back to Old Burlington Street. He bounced into Cherry's office and got his requests in before she had a chance to distract him with her long list of work matters.

'Get me a party organiser, and a caterer, and tell them I want to throw a party for the first weekend of Katy's school holidays. Get me Katy, Emily, Roger and Carolyn on the phone, preferably one at a time.'

He then went into his office and sat still for a few moments before seizing the rest of the day. His office was very different to Angela's. It was dark and cool, whereas Angela's was warm and light. The furniture was mahogany, which provided a nice contrast to the pale blue walls. Simon had a weakness for pale blue, and had insisted that they redecorate his office with his favourite colour as soon as he moved into it several years ago. The one relief to the expanse of blue came from a striking painting by Ben Johnson of the corner of an office building with venetian blinds at the window. In shades of blue and brown, the picture blended in with the room's colour scheme.

Simon looked up at the painting and thought about Angela's light airy office, and the feeling of warm relaxation he had enjoyed there. I've loved pale blue all my life, he mused, but suddenly I'm beginning to find it a bit cool. Although this office is beautiful and tasteful, it's ever so slightly depressing. Well, the office and the colours haven't changed, so perhaps I have.

Simon's reflective state was shattered a few moments later when Mike Samson, the sales director, walked into his office. A few days previously, Simon had asked him to book a meeting for the two of them to discuss one of Mike's team members, the regional head of sales for Europe, Eric Mendez. Eric's role was a critical one in the Andecis organisation, and in his recent tour of the company Simon had heard tell of a series of disasters in Eric's camp. Mike shared Simon's concerns about Eric.

Mike sank into one of the plush leather armchairs and tried unsuccessfully to put his long legs tidily in front of him. He was six foot five inches tall and as awkward and uncoordinated as a young giraffe. Simon couldn't help smiling with a degree of tenderness as he watched him.

Mike gave Simon the background to the problems. 'The guy is highly motivated and loyal, almost to the point of desperation. But he seems to totally lack judgement. Things go along smoothly for a while, and then he drops a clanger. The most recent problem was that dreadful article in the *Independent* revealing the low morale in the sales team at Andecis. Now Eric was not directly responsible for this, but he commissioned a report by our internal organisational development consultants, and was careless with its circulation. It therefore inevitably got into the wrong hands and made its way to a reporter from the paper.'

'Why was the report commissioned in the first place?' asked Simon.

'It was part of an effort on Eric's part to improve morale in his team, which fell to an all-time low after we failed to get Evereadiness through the regulators.'

'It seems to me that you might have to let him go. We can't afford to have people who lack judgement at the head of such key functions.'

'Interestingly morale on the team does seem to be improving slowly. Maybe we should let it go a little longer.' Mike shifted his long legs to an equally ungainly position.

'Haven't there been a whole string of poor judgement calls?'

'Yes. The month before the article in the *Independent* he made a speech at a retirement party which contained lewd jokes in such poor taste that by lunchtime the next day they were all around the company. He lost some credibility as a leader by doing that. Each time something like this happens I give it to him in the neck, but the effect only seems to last a short time. Just as I'm beginning to relax he comes up with something new and ingeniously awful.'

'Sack the man!' Simon gave in to a sense of righteous indignation at the thought of Eric's antics.

'I still prefer to give him another chance. Sacking him now while morale is improving would set the team back to square one.'

'OK, but keep an eye on him and let him know that he needs to learn or leave.'

After Mike left Simon thought about Eric for a while. What is it that impels an otherwise able executive to make such stupid mistakes? It's not as if he's immature, he must be nearly forty years old, Simon mused. Then in a flash of insight he compared Eric with himself. I know I have a better track record than Eric, but in Piers's eyes I keep making appalling blunders too. The press exposure over Grace Lee was worse in some ways than that article in the *Independent*. And yet Piers has given me a chance, and he's even given me a coach.

As was often the case, thinking about Piers seemed to summon him up. Cherry called to say that she had Piers on the line.

'What are you doing making phone calls at five forty-five am your time?' asked Simon, though he was not really surprised.

'It's two forty-five my time,' said Piers. 'I'm in San Francisco, and I have too much on my mind to sleep.'

'I'm sorry if I'm the cause of your insomnia.'

'Only partly the cause. First the good news. I've been hearing some good things about you. They are pleased over there that you've been busting your ass, travelling around and trying to gee up the teams. The bad news is that some people are really fed up with you. Doug Allen is close to giving up, which come to think of it may be no bad thing. However David Jones is saying that he doesn't believe you can deliver on your promises, and if things don't change sooner rather than later he won't even give you six months. That would be a disaster.'

'What a two-faced bastard! Thanks for the tip-off, I'll deal with that.' Simon's stomach started to churn. How did news like this get to Piers first and make him look like an idiot? He made such an effort to keep bad news away from Piers until he had dealt with it, yet poison seeped through the cracks however hard he tried.

'But that's not all.' Piers started to turn up the volume. 'Maybe you're the bastard, Simon. It's just got through to me that your HR team did some work which unearthed serious cultural incompatibility between Delster and Andecis before the merger. Why did you keep this from me? You shouldn't have taken a risk like that without telling me!'

Simon was stunned. He knew that Roger would not have been so disloyal as to leak that to Piers, but a disaffected member of his team could quite possibly have done so. He found himself at a loss for words.

'What's the matter, is it your tea break over there?' Piers's view of England was that everyone was always either on holiday or having a tea break.

Finally Simon felt able to say something. 'I have to admit that I didn't take it very seriously, and didn't think it worth worrying you about it at the time. It's true that cultural differences are causing problems, but Roger and I are just about to come up with some cultural integration plans to get them all working together and singing from the same hymn sheet. We can present them to you for approval when you're next here.'

Piers sighed. 'You're always running to catch up these days, Simon. It's time you started leading from the front, don't you think? And while you're at it the analysts are attacking us again. Why don't you go and speak to the financial press and ginger them up with your plans? It's the only way you'll turn things around.' Piers put the phone down, and Simon sat thinking for a minute. I don't like him but he's right. He's right about everything and it would do me no harm to do what he says. He felt even more empathy for Eric Mendez, as he realised they were having rather similar experiences at present.

He called Cherry into his office. 'Book me some meetings please with those rats from the financial news world, you know, the ones who keep pestering me for an interview. On second thoughts, fix the meetings for a day or two after my next coaching session with Angela, and make that as soon as possible.' Simon suddenly saw that if he had a firm picture of his mission, he might come over to the journalists a lot more convincingly.

Chapter Five

Simon had a chat with Katy about his plans to enrol Emily in his campaign to rebuild his relationship with Edward. Katy agreed with the plan and gave him her views on the subject.

'Edward's going through the usual adolescent thing of beginning to see his parents as flawed, and pretty embarrassing. Then you go and play straight into his hands like that, confirming all the bad things he's been thinking. He just had to cut you off and stand by his principles – when all the time he's really hurting and missing you like mad. Of course he needs his dad, but he's a boy, he'd rather die than tell you that himself.'

Where does she get all that stuff from? wondered Simon as he put the phone down. Well, I've heard it from Katy and from Angela, so maybe it's true.

These thoughts helped Simon considerably when he finally got to chat with Edward the next Saturday afternoon. Simon had been very convincing with Emily and she readily agreed to speak to Edward on his behalf. She invited Simon to visit them in Hawksbury Upton the following weekend when Edward would be home from school.

Simon used his opportunity well. He kept it short and tried not to say anything emotional or embarrassing. He just asked Edward if he would go with him to a Rugby International at Twickenham in mid-March. Edward could not bring himself to refuse; he literally beamed with joy in anticipation. 'England versus New Zealand, it couldn't be a better match! I'll definitely come.'

Simon breathed a sigh of relief. Edward was mostly quite awkward and sullen with him, but the process of healing the breach had begun. 'I'll call beforehand to agree a time to collect you from school,' said Simon, and thought to himself that Edward would now have a reason to answer his next call. He left soon afterwards, not wishing to push his luck.

On his way out Simon decided to say hello to John, the gardener. The two men sat by the fire in the gardener's cottage and exchanged news and gossip.

'By the way,' John said eventually, with a strained look on his face. 'I don't know whether this is the right thing to do, but I have something to show you that I expect you could find very helpful.' Simon's curiosity was aroused.

'I'm taking quite a risk in doing this,' John continued as he pulled a few photographs out of a drawer in the Welsh dresser. 'It might put you off me in a big way, and you may think I'm a cad. But I hope you'll appreciate why I'm showing you these.'

Simon was by now feeling rather anxious. Was it some dreadful scene of him with Grace Lee? Or was it one of his children with a paedophile? When John gave him the photographs Simon stared at them in amazement and struggled with conflicting emotions. There were six photos of Emily, naked, in the bath and in their four-poster bed in the big house.

'Who took these?'

'I did,' said John. 'Here's one more, which should make clear what was going on.' In this one John was lying on the bed, half over Emily, obviously having thrown himself there in the rush to get into the picture having set a time delay on the camera.

'We had an affair which ended last summer. I'm sorry, mate, but she made such a play for me, and it was so flattering that I couldn't resist. It was a real Lady Chatterley experience for me. It lasted six months, then she cooled off – came to her senses, I suppose. She's been careful to keep her distance since then. I took these pictures one afternoon when she was pretty drunk after some lunch party. She didn't even remember me taking them, and doesn't know of their existence. But knowing that you're struggling through the divorce as the guilty party I thought you might find them useful. Use them as you wish. I have no need of them myself.'

Simon was staggered. He had always taken Emily's fidelity for granted. He hated the idea of her having sex with anyone else. I suppose I drove her to it, he thought, but that doesn't make it any easier to cope with.

'Look, John, as you guessed this is pretty hard to take. I'm torn between breaking your front teeth, and thanking you for your thoughtfulness. I know you'd lose your job and your cottage if I showed these to Emily, so I appreciate your gesture. I'll take the photographs, although I don't know whether I'll use them. Would you give me the negatives as well?'

John handed them over willingly. As Simon drove back home he thought, damn, he probably has them on his home computer. Oh well, I'll just have to trust him not to do Emily any harm.

While Simon cruised along the motorway he had plenty of time to think. Interestingly, despite the shock of seeing the photographs, his thoughts were positive. 'Humans have on average 90,000 thoughts in a day, and most of those are negative. Think of the power of turning those thoughts into positive ones.' Angela's words at the Institute of Directors reverberated in his memory.

Well, I've been optimistic about Edward for days, and that feeling has extended to a belief that I'll sort out my personal life and gradually make it happy. Strangely, just the expectation of progress and happiness has already begun to lift my spirits. I did devote the occasional five-minute slot to focusing on the sort of peaceful, happy personal life I want. Already I'm getting some results. I'm feeling good, I've made progress with Edward, and now I've got these photos. I have mixed feelings about them, but it may help me to settle the divorce more speedily and less expensively.

Simon continued to play with the idea of showing Emily the photos and asking her to drop the claim for £2 million. She probably doesn't need the money and I would find it very hard to raise. On the other hand Emily would see it as totally unfair. This was probably her only transgression, and look how many I have to my name. It's just that in my case there was never a photographer around at a delicate moment. Can I cope with being such a hypocrite?

Simon wondered if he could get Emily to take him back by confronting her with her indiscretion. He suddenly realised that he did not want this to happen. He missed family life, the Gloucestershire home, his social life and Edward, but not Emily. He admired her, even now, and respected her, but

44

knew in his heart that he did not love her in a way that would keep him faithful. He wanted no more of that past life of secrecy and lies. He felt even happier as these revelations struck him. His future was uncertain, but he was free to live it as he chose. It felt good. The best feeling of all was to have left behind the parenting and guilt-tripping that Emily had handed out to him so freely. At the age of forty-five, Simon was growing up.

The following Monday Simon had dinner with Roger, the human resources director and his best buddy at Andecis, at the Bombay Brasserie, mainly to indulge Roger's love of Indian food. They were friendly and informal with each other but the agenda was focused on business. Sitting in wicker chairs in the elegant front room, so evocative of the British Raj, they fell to discussing Roger's ideas for cultural integration.

'We'll need a pretty large-scale programme of workshops,' said Roger.

'What levels in the organisation are you aiming at?' asked Simon.

'I think it'll have to be middle and senior management. We need to get to the people who have leverage and can bring others along with them.'

'You'll meet a lot of resistance,' said Simon. 'I think we'll have to start at the top, at the operating board, then cascade it down.'

'You're probably right,' Roger agreed. 'I'll work on a plan and give you some costings. You can have it in a week or two – I've already got it in draft.'

At this point they were ushered into the dining room in the conservatory, where the tropical effect was rather marred by the light drizzle dripping on the glass roof above.

'We'll just have to pretend it's the monsoon season,' said Simon, tucking into his Chicken Madras. Very soon he was suffering. His face became rather red, and he kept having to blow his nose. The curry was too hot for him. However he manfully ate his way through to the last grain of rice, and washed it down with a pint of Kingfisher lager. He then slumped back in his chair and tried not to belch. When he had recovered enough to speak he said: 'By the way, don't hang about with that cultural integration plan, Piers is on the warpath again.'

Simon told Roger about his recent conversation with Piers and about the leaked news of the survey showing cultural incompatibility between Delster and Andecis. Roger was shocked. 'I have no idea who would have spoken to Piers about that. I could find out, and I probably will, but maybe there's something else we should be focusing on.'

'What's that?' asked Simon.

'Our decision to keep it from him in the first place. I know you try to keep him from interfering and making impetuous decisions, which spoil our plans. But he always seems to find out, and wrong-foot you. Maybe you need to think of a better way of managing him.'

'I know. I'm going to put that on my coaching agenda with Angela. I need to be more open and collaborative with Piers. How to do it without him totally overwhelming me, that's the problem. In the meantime we need to rescue this demoralised company from itself, so burn some midnight oil on those integration plans.'

After his congenial dinner with Roger, Simon drove home. As he pulled up in front of his Holland Park home he looked up at it, a graceful mid-Victorian house on four floors. The exterior walls were pale yellow with white doors and woodwork, and the windows deep and large, making the house very light in the daytime. He went in and flopped down on one of the blue leather sofas. Emily had never liked this house. She considered the interior decor to be too masculine and modern, but Simon loved it. The through room which was dining room and sitting room in one looked out on to a small back garden and beyond that on to four acres of communal grounds. He flicked an internal switch which illuminated the garden and immediately got the impression of being outside on this winter evening.

He relaxed for a while, staring at the large gilt Buddha on the floor just in front of the French windows. It was a new acquisition. The children had pooled together and bought it for him as a Christmas present. Emily had sniffed when he opened it on Christmas morning sitting on the floor beside the Christmas tree. 'I think that belongs in your Holland Park house,' she had said, meaning that it would be out of place among the antiques in their Gloucestershire home. Simon, though, rather liked it. The children had given him a

Buddhist card with it, instead of a Christmas card, with the message 'Kindness is my religion'. Simon considered for a moment whether the children had been trying to tell him something before he noticed that the message light was flashing on the phone. He picked it up and listened.

A very sexy, husky voice with a slightly French accent announced that she would adore to organise his party for him on March the twenty-sixth. 'Just phone me back whenever you get in,' the voice said. 'My name is Sabine Duprey and I'm an insomniac, you won't disturb me.'

Do I want to do business with an insomniac with a sexy French accent? Simon asked himself. Yes, I think I do!

Sabine Duprey turned out to be even better than his fantasies, although considerably less manageable. She turned up to meet him at his house one evening a few days later wearing a low-cut top and a short skirt. In fact she looked like a French version of Grace Lee, and warning bells rang in Simon's head as she walked in through his front door, trying to be elegantly French, but tripping on his doormat. However she had something that Grace had seriously lacked, and that was a sense of humour and an ability to laugh at herself.

'Oh, silly me,' she said as she just managed to save herself from sprawling on the marble-tiled hall floor. 'Whenever I want to make a good impression I do just the opposite.'

They had an amusing evening together planning the party and agreeing the menu. They argued over everything, and in the end Sabine won on every point. They did this while drinking a bottle of champagne, which Simon had opened to celebrate the first evening he had spent with a pretty girl other than Katy since New Year's Day. Sabine did not hold her drink well. She became more and more frivolous and silly, and the French accent got thicker and thicker as the evening wore on. Finally Simon was able to get her out of the house at midnight, protesting tiredness.

Strangely enough his thoughts, as he tried to sleep that night, were not about Sabine, but Emily. He knew he had a decision to make about the divorce settlement, and whether or not to use the photographs to his advantage. Faced with a real moral dilemma he decided to talk to Angela about it on the phone the next day.

After telling her the story he said, 'I know I can use these photographs to get her to drop her claim for the £2 million.'

'Do you feel comfortable about doing that?' asked Angela.

'No, I don't. But the alternatives are not good for me financially. I can use legal means to reduce her claim, but only by about a quarter at most. And the more I use lawyers, the bigger the bill anyway, so I could end up paying the same amount.'

'Are there any other options?'

'I could just give in and pay the £2 million.'

'Where would that leave you?'

'Quite badly off, relatively speaking. It would be a mistake to cash in my Andecis shares at present, the price is too low. I suppose I could sell the pig farm and borrow against the Holland Park house. Interest rates are high just now so the cost of a big loan would be prohibitive.'

'Would it alter your lifestyle in any way?'

Simon thought for a minute. 'No, to be truthful it wouldn't.'

'I've made the point before, that creators of our own reality as we are, we have the choice of seeing the universe as a place of scarcity, or as a place of plenty,' Angela said. 'When you give with love, and without fear, it usually comes back to you in spades, especially if you don't give in order to get.'

'So maybe I should just let Emily have the £2 million?'

'How do you feel about that? Do you think she deserves it? Do you grudge it her?'

'Actually, when I stop to think about it I'd rather she had something substantial from me as a way of saying thank you. She did launch me into this glamorous world I now inhabit. I don't think I'd be here without her. She has always been a very fair person. Even though she is wealthy in her own right, she probably thinks that this two million is her due. She may have a point.'

'Then why not just let her have it? Your only other real option is to use the photographs, and then you'd have to find a way to live with yourself after doing that.'

'It's just that it goes against the grain to give money away when I don't have to. It feels as natural to me to hold on to my wealth as it feels to make it.'

Angela waited expectantly, exuding confidence that Simon would, with her support, talk his way through to a sound decision. Her positive regard seemed to travel across the telephone wires; Simon felt his energy rise and his head clear. He looked at the small picture of Katy and Edward on his desk. What would they say about me if I used the photographs? he pondered. The answer was right there in his head: 'Mean, hypocritical, bullying, user of double standards.' Do I need £2 million enough to lose the respect of my children?

'I'm not quite ready to make a decision,' Simon said eventually, 'but you've reminded me to trust in the bounty of the universe. I hope that'll give me the courage to do the right thing.'

A few days later, after some more deep consideration, Simon instructed his lawyers and accountants to sell the pig farm and raise the extra £700,000 by mortgaging the house. He went to see Emily the following weekend, and told her of his decision. He was gracious about it and said he was sorry that it had taken him so long to think it through. Emily was delighted, and kissed him goodbye when he left. Having made the decision he had no more worries about it. Every time he looked at his bank statements he said to himself: 'The universe will make sure I have every thing I need.' Katy and Edward were pleased that things were settled, and Angela thought well of him when he told her.

'You're turning into a good man, Simon,' she said. 'And it suits you.'

They both laughed but Simon felt a glow of well-being. 'I like the idea of being a good man and doing the right thing by other people,' he told her. 'It feels better and less stressful than worrying about number one all the time.'

Angela smiled. 'Aristotle understood just what you're feeling: "A man is not a good man at all who feels no pleasure in noble actions", he said.'

'I wonder how many drachma it cost him?' Simon responded. 'Only joking, Angela. Seriously, this feels like the best decision I've made in a long time.'

A few nights later he faced another make-or-break decision. He'd had an early supper at home, and then decided to spend the rest of the evening in the sauna and steam room in his basement. After half an hour of this he wrapped a large towel round his waist and came up to the kitchen for a glass of water. He heard the doorbell ringing furiously. It was Sabine. 'Where have you been? I have been ringing ze bell for hours.' Simon could tell from the thickness of her accent that she had already had a few drinks.

'I'm sorry, I was in the sauna and didn't hear the bell until just now.'

'In ze sauna? How wonderful! I will join you there.' She banged the front door shut, then marched down the stairs removing her clothes and throwing them on to the floor as she went. Simon followed, collecting up her clothes, and found himself making some pretty quick decisions about whether he wanted what was likely to follow. Slightly to his surprise he found himself thinking, No, I don't want any more relationships with wacky women like Sabine and Grace.

He took Sabine by the shoulders and, trying hard not to look at her pretty pinkish-brown nipples, said, 'Look. You are a very lovely woman, and at another time in my life we could have had a wonderful time together. Just now however I'm recovering from a broken marriage. I'm afraid I'm going to have to ask you to get dressed and go home.'

'But oh, darling, I would so love to make you feel very much better!'

It took all of Simon's wit and experience as an authoritative captain of industry to get Sabine back to the front door and out of the house. When she left he sank back into the steam room with his glass of water and found that he was shaking. Three months ago I would have been a goner, and would have allowed another neurotic troublemaker into my life. Now I am beginning to see that I have a choice, and I don't need to be the helpless pawn of every temptress who crosses my path. I think I'll wait a bit until someone more appropriate comes my way. Because they will, if I believe that one day it's going to happen.

At this very moment Angela was brushing her teeth and trying to tell her husband Geoff about Simon. She wasn't as articulate as usual because her mouth was full of toothpaste.

'It's wonderful to shee a mun grow in stature and shelf-esteem through taking such a courageous moral decision.'

'I can just about understand you. Why don't you wait till you've finished your teeth?'

'All done. It inspired me, you know, to see him make that decision to part with such a large sum of money and then feel good about it. I'm sure it will prove to be the first of many unselfish choices. It somehow raised my ethical standards too.'

'Well, don't get too high and mighty or you'll think you're too angelic for sex.'

'No chance!' said Angela, diving into bed and proving him wrong.

Chapter Six

Simon took Roger's plans for cultural integration with him to his next meeting with Angela. After reading it she said, 'It looks fine, but I suspect that you could do more.'

'What do you mean?'

'It only addresses one aspect of the problems facing the company. The tension between the Andecis and Delster methods isn't the only reason why you're experiencing delays and demoralisation. It looks to me as if you're having a crisis of leadership in Andecis. You are going to need a broader programme that transforms the company and its response to change, and that transformation must start with you.'

Simon felt slightly taken aback by this challenge until he remembered his last conversation with Piers. 'You're always running to catch up, Simon,' Piers had said. 'Lead from the front, it's the only way you'll turn things around.' Simon reflected for a while, looking at the pictures and family photographs on the walls of the bright cheerful office. He particularly liked the picture of Angela on the beach, with her four children sitting all over her. It had a way of putting him in a good mood and reminding him that there was more to life than Andecis. Angela meanwhile waited patiently for him to absorb her remarks.

'I guess that when I started this coaching programme I accepted that I would have to face up to some personal change.'

'Simon, people are always learning and changing. My role is to help you to do it in a self-aware way, and to have some say in the direction. If you want to transform the company, you first of all have to transform yourself. That's not as hard as you might think, and it can be a very rewarding process. What provides the fuel and direction is knowing your mission and purpose in life. Remember how I've been saying that with a mission to work towards the universe will help you to realise your dreams and aspirations?'

'Behind everything you say, Angela, is the premise that we create our own reality. I'm just beginning to see how that can happen in my personal life – by the way, I did what you suggested and am back in touch with Edward.' Simon beamed as he gave this news.

'That's wonderful! How did you manage it?'

'I bribed him with tickets to a Rugby International at Twickenham.'

'That was ingenious of you! You must be so relieved, Simon. Why, it's a weight off my mind just to hear the news!'

'I can't tell you how pleased I am to have him back in my life, even if it's only at the other end of a telephone line so far. It feels like a miracle, but I know you'd say that I brought it about by creating my own reality. I must admit I've still only the vaguest idea of how we do that, and why it's possible. To put it into practice to transform the business and my style of leadership I'll have to understand it a whole lot better.'

'OK. I'll have a go at explaining it. Are you sitting comfortably? This could take a few hours.'

'I can give you half an hour.'

'Then that will have to do. Here we go. The Western view of science, until the surprising discoveries of the quantum physicists in the early twentieth century, was pretty straightforward. Scientists thought that we live in a material world, made up of a multitude of separate objects assembled into a huge machine. Descartes influenced us to see a dual universe, where mind is separate from matter. Most of us in the West, despite a century of quantum physics, still see ourselves as separate beings in a material world. To get what we want we have to fight, master, protect our gains from enemies around every corner, control and dominate.

'Yet the first thirty years of the twentieth century changed our understanding of physics radically. It showed us that the solid material reality, which we thought made up our world, is an illusion. The search for the building blocks of the universe led to the splitting of the atom and then to deeper and deeper penetration into an amazing subatomic world. This search for the ultimate stuff of the universe showed us that there isn't any! The more we penetrate into the sub-microscopic world, the more we discover that the universe is composed of interacting and connected components, constantly in motion, constantly changing. There is nothing solid there.

'We discovered that mass is nothing but a form of energy. Even an object at rest has energy stored in its mass. Everything is energy. Nothing is solid. Under a microscope every seemingly solid object shows itself to be alive with vibrating molecules, moving at a little less than the speed of light, thus appearing to us to be solid. Energy, and only energy, is the basic stuff of the universe.

'Look at your arm. It seems solid, doesn't it? Yet inside that arm, inside every part of your body, there's a very different state to what we imagine. Subject your cells to a subatomic investigation and you find that you're mostly composed of space!'

'Hang on a minute, Angela. I learnt all this stuff at university a long time ago, but in an abstract sort of a way. It suddenly becomes very personal when I apply this thinking to my own body. This arm does seem very solid, and I know that if I cut it open it would be full of tissues, blood and bone.' Simon's tone was half joking, half serious.

'It's at the subatomic level that it's mostly empty space, not at the macroscopic level that you can see.'

'So inside of this tissue,' said Simon, pinching himself, 'is just a whole load of hot air.'

Angela smiled at him. 'That's the case, I'm afraid. Inside this space that's your arm are atoms, tiny drops separated by huge distances. Inside the atoms in the vast space between nuclear drops the electrons are whizzing about. They make up the tiniest fraction of the total mass of your arm, but their ferociously rapid movement gives it its solid appearance.'

'So it's the vibrating electrons that create the impression that this arm of mine is solid?' Simon looked at his arm again, trying to imagine it as a swarming mass of little shooting stars instead of the lump of flesh it appeared to be.

'That's so. Not only are you composed mostly of empty space, but the subatomic particles inside of you are constantly changing,' Angela continued, warming to her theme. 'All particles can be changed into other particles. They can be created from energy and can vanish into energy. These particles don't exist on their own; they can only be seen as an integrated part of the whole. Particles can only be observed in movement and interaction with their surrounding environment.

'A further discovery by Heisenberg and his buddies is that you, as an observer of nature, can only understand the properties of subatomic objects through your interaction with them. There's nothing objective out there. We can never speak about nature without at the same time speaking about ourselves. The world is subjective, not objective, and we're intimately tied up with it. We can never be objective observers of nature. By observing we change.

'Our consciousness, our understanding, our perceptions and our intentions play a crucial role in physical reality. We change it. We create it. The true solid stuff of the universe is energy, but it's conscious energy, expressing itself in many forms. All energy is conscious. All matter, which is really a form of energy, is conscious.

'The material aspect of a substance only exists when someone is present to observe it. At other times it remains a wave of pure potentiality. Our thoughts control whether a potentiality turns into a "material" object or a "concrete" event. If you believe in a potential future you influence or even create that future. You can make it happen.'

'Can I really create more or less any future I want?'

'You do constantly. Innumerable times a day you make decisions that alter the future, and sometimes the present. You're always making choices about what you expect, what you want or what you fear, and these choices affect what happens.'

'It seems an enormous responsibility.'

'We make these choices unconsciously much of the time. So it doesn't appear to most of us that we're responsible. As David Bohm said, "Thought creates reality and then says I didn't do it".'

'That's a truly wonderful quote.'

'We choose which experiences to create. We have our beliefs, our hopes and fears, our intentions and these all lead us to choose what we want and what we expect. Now

55

that we know how all of this works we can make these choices consciously. If we remain unconscious of the process we continue to wield this enormous creative power irresponsibly.'

'So if I become clear about my mission in life, and create in my mind the sort of future I want and expect, then that'll be a responsible way of using my creative power?' Simon leant forward, looking excitedly at Angela.

'And what's more your positive expectations will make it much more likely you achieve what you want.' Angela poured them both a cup of tea while Simon sat lost in thought for a few moments.

'I'm inclined to agree with your reasoning, Angela,' he said eventually. 'After all, quantum mechanics is the most proven theory in the history of physics. We're surrounded by its products in modern life, from laser beams to plastic products to computer chips, just to name a few.'

'Yes, it's strange that we humans are still so inclined to base our beliefs on scientific theories that were found wanting a hundred years ago.'

'I guess I have to be patient about discovering my mission in life. It's something I've been thinking about lately, I'm not sure why. Maybe it's about the legacy I'll leave. Less money than I'd thought, that's for sure, but what else? It's beginning to matter to me that I leave something of value behind when I die. And I'm not just talking about material things.' Simon looked pensive as he said this.

'Let me ask you a few questions to get you started on thinking it through. What's special and unique about you?'

'Although I'm painfully aware of my shortcomings, especially right now, I've always been clear about what it is I bring to the party. I have a lot of organising ability. I've a way of making things happen, sometimes admittedly leaving a lot of bruised people in my path. I'm quite clear-sighted, when I've worked things out. Once I form a view that a thing is both desirable and possible, I do galvanise people into action to make it happen. I guess I've been good at creating my own reality. But I've done it the hard way, by creating a hostile world that I've had to fight against to carve out my achievements. I would say I'm both a healthcare scientist and a businessman. I made sure I got experience in marketing, business strategy and corporate finance as I worked my way up. I'm a leader with many strings to my bow, but a dominating and controlling one in your book, I dare say.'

Angela ignored the disparaging remarks that were mixed in with the list of strengths. 'So, you're a clear-sighted experienced leader who organises, galvanises into action and controls to achieve your goals. OK. What do you really enjoy? What gives you immense pleasure and satisfaction? Are you in the healthcare sector by chance, or because you like it?'

'Because I like it. In fact I chose to do science at school and university because it fascinates me. I stayed in the healthcare sector even after I became a general manager and business leader because I felt it was how I wanted to contribute to the world. But I don't think I was being altruistic. I saw this sector as the stage for the making of my fortune. What gives me a buzz now is bringing a product to the market that can save lives, or improve the quality of life for thousands or even millions of people. I also get a buzz out of creating and building organisations to make this possible.'

'Then you're already on the right path for achieving your purpose. Do you think that doing what gives you this buzz could be why you're here on earth? Could this be your mission?'

'Yes, I see that now as I talk to you about it. But something's missing. It's very contaminated with my personal anxieties over status, wealth and achievement. I feel so anxious all the time about protecting what I've gained so far. I keep seeing it all slip away in my mind, rather like my marriage and family life have done.'

'That could be remedied by a shift of focus. Right now, you're probably doing what you're here on earth to do, and finding it rewarding. However you've been focusing so hard on what you want to get from it all that you're spoiling your pleasure and enjoyment. If you can focus instead on what you want to give, to the company and to the world, you might find it all gets a lot easier.'

Simon looked uncomfortable and shifted restlessly in his chair. 'I worry that if I don't look out for myself and my own career nobody else will.'

'That viewpoint can only be valid if you stick to the old-fashioned Newtonian idea of humans as separate isolated cogs in a hostile unpredictable world. Can you see it any other way?'

'I guess I'm coming round to half believing that this is a universe of plenty if we choose to see it like that.'

'To add to that, when you're acting out your purpose in life, the universe swings into motion to support you in achieving that purpose. The more you choose to be of service, the more profoundly you experience that support. If you're clear about your mission, and take whatever risks are necessary to follow your passion and enthusiasm, then everything else will fall into place. You'll make money readily, and it will feel enjoyable and effortless.'

'So you're saying that if I focus on my mission to save lives, improve quality of life and build organisations to do that, then I don't need to worry about myself. The universe will make sure that I have whatever I need to achieve my purpose.'

'Absolutely.'

'But suppose the universe decides that I can achieve that purpose living in a three-bedroom 1960s town house in Staines, eating takeaway curries at night!'

They both laughed a long time.

'I know you don't believe that will ever happen to you,' said Angela, 'But have another cup of tea to sustain you just in case it does.'

'I want an answer, you can't fob me off with a cup of tea.'

'Come on, I know you know the answer. You have recently given away £2 million because you believe that you live in a universe of plenty.'

'OK. I'm being a bit slow here. It's just hit me. If the universe is really one big thought then there can be no scarcity, poverty or takeaway curry existences unless I seriously believe that will be my experience.'

'That's right,' said Angela. 'If you choose to believe in a universe of plenty then you can continue to live in your Victorian house in Elgin Crescent, or maybe in Buckingham Palace if that's more convenient for the office. If you believe in a world of scarcity then you'll manufacture scarcity around you because that is your basic thought. No matter what you get, it'll never be enough. When you have a mission, and you want to serve instead of take, your core belief is that there's so much abundance, you can afford to give it away, and you'll never go short. The unconscious mind takes its cue from our core beliefs and manufactures situations that reflect them.

Our willingness to serve and to give directs the universe to give to us.'

'I have to go now. We haven't worked on your idea of a leadership transformation programme yet, but you've got me to first base for transforming Simon Bruce.'

'Yes, any plans you make will be all the more powerful if they're based on moving you towards your mission in life. We should meet again soon and work on those plans.'

'I need to do some more thinking about this mission of mine. It's still too diffuse, I must sharpen it up somewhat. However, you've got me started and given me plenty of food for thought.'

'Chat it over with your friends and colleagues,' said Angela. 'Remember you don't have to achieve everything on your own.'

Simon walked back to his office on automatic pilot. Lost in thought, he noticed nothing going on around him in the narrow streets of St James's. He felt very excited about the idea that he had a mission in life, that he was here on earth for a purpose, and that he was getting close to discovering what it was. I'm a bag of hot air with the power to create the universe, he amused himself by thinking. After bumping into a tourist in the Burlington Arcade he returned to the world outside him, and was able to concentrate on his voicemails when he got back to his office. One of these was rather unexpected. It said: 'This is Inspector Spencer Larkman from Scotland Yard. Could you call me please on a matter of the utmost importance.'

The implied menace in the message meant that he phoned the inspector right away.

Inspector Larkman had some worrying news for him. 'I'm sorry to have to tell you this, sir, but you have just received an honour I'm sure you could do without. You have arrived, so to speak, as far as the animal rights campaigners are concerned. You are now on Red Roger's death list.'

Simon felt like he had been hit in the stomach. He had been in the bad books of the animal rights campaigners all of his working life, despite the fact that he had been instrumental in reducing animal testing in Andecis to a bare essential minimum. However, he had never been on a death list before. Happy thoughts of his mission flew out of his mind, and a knot of anxiety formed at the back of his throat. Red Roger was someone the police were taking very seriously indeed. They were sure he had been involved in a recent spate of letter and car bombings. No one had been killed, but some people had been badly injured. As yet they had no hard evidence with which to charge him, but felt the need to warn and protect his intended victims.

'I'm afraid we will have to provide you with police surveillance at your home, I mean your homes. In our opinion your wife and children are in danger as well. If I could arrange a meeting with you I will go through all the precautionary steps we consider necessary.'

Chapter Seven

While Simon and Inspector Larkman were discussing security at his home in Holland Park that evening, Red Roger was discussing Simon with his three supporters in the garage of his house in Birmingham. Red Roger was thin and wiry, with rather straggly reddish-brown hair which hung in wisps over his collar. His most arresting features were his dark and deep-set eyes, which had a way of staring right through you as if you didn't exist. The only people who existed for Red Roger were his intended victims, whom he hated with a passion, his fellow activists, the police and his girlfriend. His world was very narrow, but he had a mission in life, and he allowed no distraction to divert him from his cause. His uncle, also an animal rights activist, had died in prison on a hunger strike many years ago. As a very young man Red Roger had decided to avenge his favourite relative, and to devote himself to ending cruelty to animals in the laboratories.

This year had started badly for Red Roger. His fanaticism, and inclination to be unstable, had eventually proved too much for the leadership of the Birmingham branch of the animal rights movement. After a dramatic blow-up, in which he had been told he was more of a hindrance than a help, he severed ties with the 'official' organisation. This had happened on New Year's Day, at about the same time that Simon's personal life had fallen apart. At first Red Roger saw the split from the official movement as a disaster. His inadequacy and psychological instability left him ill-equipped for normal work, and his 'career' as an activist was all he had. However, his fanaticism propelled him forward and he set up his own tiny organisation, with three supporters. Thus he carried on with his campaigns without the constant inter-ference of his more conservative ex-colleagues. In the end he thought he might actually be better off, but he continued to feel outraged by the rejection.

The three supporters, Fred, Kevin and Tom, were slightly less single-minded, but very loyal to Red Roger. They had many disagreements over tactics and strategy, but stayed together through thick and thin. Tonight they were discussing their death list.

'I'm not sure why you've added Simon Bruce to it,' said Tom. 'We usually go for the senior scientists who are directly involved in animal testing.'

'Well, we've blown off a few of their limbs in the past, but they continue to maim and torture animals just the same,' said Fred. 'I would imagine you're trying to up the ante, aren't you, Red?'

'I should think it would be bloody obvious,' growled Red Roger. 'Big names mean big publicity, you dimbos.'

'That's all very well, but it also means a big increase in police activity to stop us in our tracks.' Kevin was inclined to be cautious.

'Don't be such a wimp, they have nothing on us. Let Simon Bruce stew over this for a while, then when he's getting really jumpy, we'll do something. It won't do these bastards any harm to experience some of the fear they cause helpless animals.'

'I thought we were trying to get publicity, not revenge,' snapped Kevin.

'Come on, let's go to the pub,' said Fred. 'The new list is out and Simon Bruce is on it so there's no point arguing about it.' Everyone saw reason and went with him round the corner to the White Swan.

Simon somehow managed to put Red Roger to the back of his mind and carried on with his attempts to sort out the current problems in Andecis. However at his next meeting with Angela he found himself discussing the death threat.

'It seems as if I've pulled something quite nasty into my life,' he said after telling her about it all. 'I feel quite over-awed by the responsibility of being the person who creates my own reality. Clearly there are innumerable possible futures out there for me, depending on what I choose to believe and expect. How can I wield this power for the best? I've obviously had some dark belief in the past which has brought about this menace from the animal rights crowd. It's hard enough sometimes to make a simple decision like what clothes to put on in the morning, or to believe that I'm going to win the next point in a tennis game. Where do I go for the considerably more important question of how to create a good future through today's thoughts and actions?' The strain and worry showed on Simon's face.

Angela smiled. 'Don't worry, there are ways to get guidance, but first of all let me reassure you that there's no right choice or wrong choice. Each path you might take will have a set of lessons for you. Life is really about learning.'

Simon groaned. 'I've done so much painful learning lately, I think I'm quite justified in wanting to know how to make choices that cause me to learn in more pleasant and enjoyable ways.'

'That's a reasonable aspiration,' said Angela. 'You can actually get guidance from your intuition if you listen to it. This guidance comes in the form of impulses to do one thing or another.'

'I don't know if I trust my impulses,' said Simon. 'They've led me up some pretty dark alleyways in the past.'

'Well, maybe you had some lessons to learn by exploring those dark alleyways. But you do have a point. You need to learn to distinguish between impulsive desires, some of which are destructive, and your intuition, which is always constructive.'

'How do I do that?'

'Both can feel compelling. A good guiding rule is this – don't act out of a sense of urgency. Impulses are a strong burst of energy, followed by quiet. They come on strong and then fade away. Your intuition, your wise inner knowing, blossoms over time and subtly influences your direction. There's always time to reflect before acting. If a thought unhurriedly returns to you three times or more, then that's your intuition speaking to you. If it's important you won't forget it.'

'I have so little practice in listening to my intuition,' said Simon. 'My scientific and management training has taught me to rely on intellect and logic for making decisions.'

'Is that how you chose Grace Lee?'

Simon laughed. 'You see what happens when I go by my impulses!'

'That was probably an impulsive desire, rather than an example of wise loving guidance from your intuition. Intuitive messages are persistent, but not urgent. They don't usually demand immediate action, and are rarely radical without smaller steps to initiate change. These messages are usually loving, reassuring, encouraging and positive.'

'The decision to merge with Delster and Zeus felt like that. Once I formed the idea, it didn't feel urgent, but it wouldn't go away. Probably if I'd relied on intellect and logic alone I wouldn't have bought both companies at more or less the same time.'

'So you *can* hear your intuition. You know, you can't stop your intuition from working, but you do sometimes stop yourself from hearing it. It speaks to you all the time, but if you have turbulent emotions, like anger, sadness, jealousy or vengefulness, they act like storm waves and drown the sound of your inner voice. The best advice I ever had was to refrain from taking decisions or actions when you're in the grip of these emotions. The same goes for all the painful emotions: regret, guilt and shame. Acknowledge them and let them go. Then you can tune in to your intuition.'

'Is that the only source of guidance?'

'You can also get a steer from the meaningful coincidences that crop up in your life. You know, the people and opportunities that show up just when you need them, and seem to take you forward to your goals.'

'Like you, Angela!'

'Like me, Simon. If I can just go back to quantum physics for a moment, these meaningful coincidences tell us that the universe is responding to our thoughts and expectations. This is the process for creating the chance opportunities that move us along. So another way of getting guidance is to note these coincidences, and map them to see which way they're leading you.'

'OK, I'll try to take note of both my intuitive messages and the coincidences and what they seem to be telling me about direction. As far as Red Roger is concerned, my impulse tells me to panic and go to live in Siberia, but my intuition is quietly and persistently telling me to follow the security measures and stay alert.'

'There you are. I'd be rather sad if you ran off to Siberia. The formula is to follow your intuition, and picture and expect the sort of safe future you want. Maybe this death threat is just an opportunity for you to learn to do that. Heisenberg taught us that as our perception of an object changes, the object itself literally alters. Our greatest tool for changing the world is to change our mind about the world.

'What gives us this huge creative power is the connected-ness of everything in the universe. We seem to be separate beings, but in truth at the subatomic level, in the world of vibrating and ever-changing particles, we are joined-up parts of the energy and consciousness of the universe. Together we are all one big dynamic thought. If you forget this and trust only in your own individual strength then you are very weak and have every reason to panic.'

Just then the fire alarm went off, interrupting their discussion. They sat still for a while, hoping it was a false alarm, but when it proved persistent, and they noticed people walking past Angela's office door to the exit, they gave in to the inevitable and followed them out into the street. 'Another bloody bomb scare,' said the porter as they crowded past him. 'What times we live in.'

'This is very exciting,' said Simon. 'It gives me a chance to see who else is here being coached.' They followed the crowd down Ryder Street to a gathering point in a yard between two buildings where they stood around for quite a while; Simon looked around him but spotted no other captains of industry. While they were waiting Simon started a conversation with Angela.

'I've just had a thought. Can I make you a bad coach by thinking you're a bad coach?'

This question took Angela by surprise. 'Hmm,' she replied. 'You can certainly pull a bad coach into your life if you've a set of beliefs that says coaches are bad. Or if you believe that you're unlucky and tend to pull the short straw, then you're more likely to choose a coach who turns out to be bad for you.'

'But could I actually make you perform badly as a coach by expecting you to fail?'

'I think you could,' said Angela. 'Your negative expect-ations would reach my mind at an unconscious level, and programme me to do all the wrong things as far as you're concerned.'

'That's interesting. Actually I have read that if a teacher has low expectations of a student, then the student can never get beyond the limitations set in that teacher's mind. I suppose that's another example of the same process at work. In the same way a manager can limit the performance of a subordinate.'

The crowd started to wander back to the office, the bomb scare over. Simon and Angela followed. When they returned to Angela's office she continued with her point.

'Everything that happens, we make happen through our thoughts; they decide which of an infinite number of possible events will actually occur in our reality. Through this huge network of energy waves, that connects us to everyone and everything, we pull whatever we believe will happen into our lives. Nothing takes place by chance. Even seemingly disastrous setbacks have been engineered by our unconscious minds, searching for a way to help us to learn and grow, so that we can reach our full potential.

'The way it happens for us as individuals is that we get mental images accompanied by strong emotions of desire or fear. These act as blueprints for the objects, conditions or events to appear in our lives. The unconscious mind, which does the attracting, does not distinguish between fears and desires, it simply works to fulfil our expectations for us. This is why it's no bad thing to focus your attention on positive expectations instead of fears and worries. Those who fear the worst attract bad luck. Those who are more optimistic are far more lucky.'

At that moment Angela's secretary put her head round the door. 'Your husband wants you to phone him, he says it's quite urgent.'

'Thanks, Mary, I'll call him as soon as this meeting's over.' Mary hesitated as if she wanted to say something more, but she thought better of it and closed the door.

Simon continued with the discussion. 'So by worrying that Grace Lee might threaten my marriage, I made it more likely that it would happen!'

'Quite possibly. Everything you can picture in your mind is already there in the universe, waiting for you to connect with it so that it can move from potential into your reality. That thing called a thought in your head is already there in the physical world. You just make it happen by thinking about it.'

'That's well put, Angela. The way you relate quantum physics to everyday experience is quite fascinating. I have another question.'

'Fire away.'

'How is it that sometimes I hope for an event fervently, and yet it doesn't happen? For example, I really wanted to see Edward but it took two months to bring that about.'

'On the physical plane our thoughts and beliefs don't manifest immediately. It might take time, and might even seem like luck or a random event when it does happen. Anyway, perhaps you weren't seeing yourself as deserving his love and company. When you think you don't deserve a thing it doesn't show up in your life even if you want it to. I imagine you were feeling pretty guilty about Grace Lee and your ejection from the family home?'

'Yes, I beat myself up a lot. I suppose that what changed the situation with Edward was that I began to get genuinely hopeful about seeing him. Also with your help I was able to see that I was important in his life. I began to see myself as his father again, not just as a guilty, undeserving rat.'

'There you are. The universe doesn't always give us what we want and expect right away. The intelligent energy in the universe sometimes seems to take a view that now is not the right time for a thing to happen. Maybe you need to grow and change first. Sometimes we have to be patient. In this case it was probably guilt that stopped you from getting what you wanted and making contact with Edward.'

Simon sat very still for a while. Edward's tear-stained face on New Year's Day came into his mind, as it had done many times before. 'Yes, I can see how my terrible feelings of guilt and shame will have temporarily created a world for me in which I was punished by Edward's rejection.'

'Well, if you have the power to do that, you also have the power to create a safe and happy future for yourself.'

'I'll work on that, Angela. And as I put less energy into worrying about the death threat, maybe I can put more into thinking about my mission and purpose!'

As soon as Simon left Angela called her husband. His secretary answered the phone and said, 'Oh yes, Mrs Jones, he asked me to interrupt him in his meeting as soon as you called, please hold on.' Angela wondered what was going on.

'Angela, thank God you've called. There's a problem at

home, and I'm in the middle of these negotiations and can't leave. Can you go home now by any chance?'

Angela thought anxiously about her children, and also about the client who was due to arrive in half an hour. 'What's the matter, Geoff?'

'It's the nanny, she's sick and can't look after Elise and Tom. Your mother's away, the older kids are at school and it's a bit of a mess.'

'She seemed fine this morning,' cried Angela, appalled at the prospect of cancelling a client meeting at short notice. 'Oh well, I guess there's no choice.' And she ran out of the office, after a quick word with Mary about rescheduling her next appointment. Sitting on the train she tried to call home but found to her dismay that her mobile phone batteries were low and she couldn't get through. Simon and I have something in common today, she thought as the train crept far too slowly along the track. We're both wondering why we bring worrying things into our lives.

When Angela got home she found the two little ones, aged three and six, busily and cheerfully looking after their beloved nanny, who was lying on the sofa in the family room looking pale and feeble.

'We're fine, Mummy,' said Elise, the six-year-old. 'You needn't have come home so early.'

Chapter Eight

The opportunity to spend some time with Carolyn came up the next week. She persuaded Simon to come with her to a global marketing conference in Paris. 'I need your backing, Simon,' she said. 'I'm presenting a major proposal for changing the emphasis and direction of our marketing effort. I know you're behind my proposals, but I could do with your support in public. You need only make a brief appearance, a couple of hours on the first afternoon will do. I'll brief you more fully on Eurostar if you travel over with me.'

Simon jumped at the opportunity. Here was a chance to get to know Carolyn better, and to get a closer look at the marketing proposals. Roger would probably tell me to stay out of the detail and leave it to the specialists, but the chance to check them out before they go live is being handed me on a plate, he thought gleefully.

On the morning of the journey, just as he was leaving the office, Simon had another phone call from Inspector Larkman, checking that he was happy with the security arrangements.

'I know it's all very intrusive,' said the inspector, 'but you could pay a big price if we aren't vigilant. Two weeks ago a senior scientist at a competitor of yours had his arm blown off by a letter bomb.'

Simon suddenly went hot and cold all over. The seriousness of the threat hit home. The thought of him, or one of the children, losing a limb was too awful to contemplate.

'I'll co-operate in any way I can,' he promised Inspector Larkman, and then ran down the stairs to the waiting taxi. Carolyn's smiling face cheered him up. She was obviously excited about the conference, and he was glad to be giving her his support.

As they had three hours together on the train Simon started first of all to chat to her about his mission, suspecting rightly that she would be a good sounding board. As soon as he finished recounting his conversation with Angela about his mission she said: 'So you're where you want to be, building businesses in the healthcare sector. When you say you get a buzz out of saving lives and improving quality of life, is there any section of the population which tugs most at your heart strings?'

'You might expect me to say children or babies, or undernourished and diseased people in Third World countries, but you'd be wrong. I do feel a desire to provide drugs for disadvantaged and vulnerable people in society, but it's the older folk who capture my sympathy the most. I've seen my father and several older relatives and family friends turn inwards, get depressed, develop chronic diseases like Alzheimer's, and generally have a bad time of it in their later years.'

'And we could all be there in the end,' said Carolyn, 'unless we die young, which is not a happy alternative.'

'Yes, it seems as if the trend for people to live longer is not a happy one for many folk,' Simon continued. 'As their bodies begin to let them down in different ways their lives close in on them. They either feel guilty about the demands they make on their younger relatives, or neglected because their children live far away, as is often the case.'

'If I'm not mistaken many of the high-profile drugs in the pipeline since the merger are aimed at this group.'

'That's true. We've got drugs for memory loss, impotence and prostate cancer, and are just breaking ground on a drug for one of the most common causes of deafness in older people. There are many others of course, but those will be the blockbusters along with the jet lag cure, and those are the ones in which I'm really interested.'

'Could it be that you're enthusiastic about these drugs because they are something to do with your purpose in life?' asked Carolyn.

'Yes, it's all coming together now. Apart from the jet lag cure, all the drugs are about improving quality of life for older people.'

'Even the jet lag cure, although it'll mostly benefit the jet-setting business community, can be a great help to older people. It can keep them travelling, getting winter sunshine and seeing far-flung relatives. You could use it as part of a package that stops their lives from closing in on them.' Carolyn, her eye on possible marketing opportunities, was getting excited.

'Yes, that hits a note. 'It's what I am really enthusiastic about: helping an ageing population to keep their memories, keep their minds clear, combat incapacitating disease, and keep on the move so that their lives can continue to be rich and rewarding. I think that older people have so much wisdom to share with us. It's a shame to lose it under layers of depression, ill health or loss of mental faculties. I guess that's why I'm chief executive of Europe for Andecis, and why it's so important to me to make a success of the merger and the drugs it brought with it.'

'Well, there you are. I think that's fantastic, Simon, I'm quite inspired.' Simon thought she was teasing him for a moment, but she carried on enthusiastically. 'The timing of this conversation is fortuitous. You know that the proposition I'm putting to the global conference is to take advantage of the Internet to market our drugs differently. Now that so many of our end customers have access to the Net, they're using it to gain knowledge about the best drugs for their various ailments.

'My best friend died of breast cancer last year. Even when she was very ill she got information from her computer about the best new drug to hit the market, and persuaded her doctor at the Royal Marsden to put her on to this drug, even though it was very expensive and her prognosis was not good. I was too wrapped up in supporting her at the time to think of the marketing implications for Andecis, but when I finally got round to it I realised that it spelt a big opportunity.'

The train emerged from the tunnel at this point and they both looked out at the flat northern French countryside as they roared past at high speed.

'You're going to propose that we start marketing to the patient by providing information and education over the Internet, aren't you?' Simon turned his attention back to Carolyn.

'That's one proposal. The other is to aim at organisations

like the Alzheimer's support group, Aids charities and Age Concern. This'll mean a big shift away from our current practice of using medical reps to sell to consultants and to general practitioners. We'll still do some of that, of course, but we have to use the power of the well-informed end user to influence what the doctor prescribes.'

'So, what's fortuitous about this conversation of ours?' asked Simon feeling very energised by Carolyn's proposal. He also noticed her animated, lively face and thought, not for the first time, how attractive she was.

'If you can spell out your mission to improve life quality for the ageing population this afternoon at the conference, then my proposals to shift our marketing effort in the direction of bodies like Age Concern can sit in that context and support your mission. In fact if you approve I may even propose that we go further. We could invest in providing information and assistance to these support groups and institutions for the aged. This would be information to improve their quality of life in all ways possible, not just advertising platforms for our drugs. Information on our drugs would be part of it, but only a part.'

'Brilliant. We can also set up a website for the over-sixties, or whatever age you think appropriate, so the population at large can have access to anything they need to keep their lives from closing down. We can offer a service providing free assistance with computer problems to encourage this age group to have home computers. We could probably get government funding for that in many countries. We can also provide a bank of computers in places where older people go to congregate, like retirement clubs.'

'I think we're on to something good,' said Carolyn. 'But we've got to watch that we don't get involved in the detail that the regional marketing teams will want to be dealing with. We must lead with vision, direction and inspiration, and leave the rest to them.'

Simon was well and truly put in his place, but Carolyn did it so charmingly that he decided to obey her meekly. 'Fine, let's leave it to the specialists, I'd rather be a visionary leader anyway,' he joked. 'You've been a great help to me today. Tell me, Carolyn, as we're talking about missions and so forth, have you worked out your own mission in life?'

'I've been working on it for a year or so with my coach,

ever since I read Angela's book. I didn't have an epiphany like you just had, it came to me more slowly. I don't have a grand mission, which will benefit millions of people world-wide. But I feel very strongly the need to work and live in a way that makes life better for the people with whom I come into contact. Angela's book taught me to focus on what I can give, rather than what I can get out of all situations. So I do put a lot of effort into developing my team, empowering them to produce great ideas, coaching individuals and giving guidance and service across the company.'

'Well, you put your money where your mouth is. Mostly when you're around the atmosphere becomes calmer and more positive. I think you have a way of making people feel better about themselves and more confident. Occasionally you seem a bit stressed out and anxious, but most of the time you're like the evening star – shining brightly but not burning!'

'Thank you for that. It's nice to be thought of as Venus.'

Simon looked at Carolyn and thought to himself that Venus had other qualities too. He wondered for a few moments whether she could be the woman he'd been waiting for. Interestingly, Carolyn was at the same time looking into Simon's dark brown eyes and thinking, help, a woman could get lost in those depths.

The train pulled into the Gare du Nord at that point, and they were whisked off to the Paris Marriott in a black stretch limousine. Their double act at the conference was well received. Carolyn looked quietly pleased but tired at the end of the day. Simon, who had watched her with interest all afternoon, found her speech was powerful and enthusiastic, but logical and convincing. She was confident, and used pauses to great dramatic effect.

She was now surrounded by a number of excited people. She has star quality, he mused, but it hasn't gone to her head. She just gets on with things, and doesn't blow her own trumpet. Yet she's quite political. It was a canny move of hers to get me here and to give her such public support. However her political behaviour felt constructive to him, focused as it was on benefits to the company, and very supportive to his aims. In no way did it seem to be something she had done solely for her own glory. The more I think about it, he said to himself, the more this focus on giving rather than getting seems to win the day. Carolyn puts her effort into achieving company goals and into helping deserving souls, and yet she doesn't lose out personally. Quite the opposite: she seems to gain huge support and respect internationally.

Simon walked over towards Carolyn, fought his way to her side, and announced to the group as a whole: 'Carolyn and I are going to have dinner together. We have to do some planning for tomorrow. If we're not too tired we'll join in on the party afterwards.' He shot Carolyn a conspiratorial glance, and she winked at him. Although he was unsure what that meant, he found he didn't care.

Simon booked them into a tiny restaurant round the corner from the hotel, away from the glitz and the crowds, where the chef was known to be good. 'I am so grateful to you,' said Carolyn, 'I'm far too tired to handle the conference party. I hope you didn't mean it when you said that we would be planning tomorrow's sessions. I would much rather talk about sex and violence or the latest good play in London, or even children.'

'Spot on. I've no intention of talking about marketing, except to say that I thought you were a superstar today.'

Carolyn blushed with pleasure at this praise. 'So were you. Together we did it.'

'Tell me a bit about yourself, Carolyn. You know all about me, I've been in the papers often enough, much to my shame on some occasions. Yet all I know about you is that you're a marketing director, with previous experience in the pharmaceutical industry, and your last job was with Procter and Gamble in Cincinnati. And of course you're an old friend of Piers. You don't seem to be married, which is a puzzle, as you're such a lovely person. Please fill in the gaps.'

Simon was actually quite stunned with Carolyn's appearance that evening. He had only seen her in power suits and tailored dresses before. She always looked well groomed, and attractive but, like Angela, not distractingly so. Tonight she was distinctly distracting. She wore a backless black dress with thin straps crossing her back and keeping the dress from gaping open and revealing her breasts, which had no visible sign of support. He could see the muscles rippling along her back, her arms and her calves. 'She's in fantastic shape,' he thought appreciatively, 'and yet she's incredibly feminine.'

Her blond hair shone in the light and her green eyes sparkled. She did not look the least bit tired any more.

'I'm a widow, actually. I married John when I was twenty-five and he forty-five.'

Quite an age gap, thought Simon.

'He brought me up really. I have two stepsons from his first marriage. I get on really well with them now, although they gave me a hard time at first. John died six years ago, of cancer, and I haven't remarried. I read history at Cambridge. I worked for McKinsey's for a few years, doing marketing consultancy, and then got a job in marketing with IFF, the perfume company. After that I went to Procter and Gamble as marketing manager, and worked my way up to vice president. They offered me a great job in the USA, and my husband took early retirement and came over with me. He started writing, which he had always wanted to do.

'We were very happy there, and he was just completing his first novel when he died, very quickly, of liver cancer. He was a great mentor for me. He was a real corporate animal, like yourself, although he never got up to board level, I don't think he was hungry enough. However I was hungry, and he saw that and helped me to rise up to quite a senior position in Cincinnati. He supported me through all the buffeting and helped me to put things into perspective and not to take them too personally.

'Six months after John died I met Piers in Grand Cayman where I was having a holiday, a retreat really. He was good and kind to me and we became friends. I didn't see him very often; no one sees Piers very often. But we got to know each other well enough so that when this job with Andecis became vacant he suggested I apply. And you know the rest.'

'I don't know all the rest. Are you in a relationship now? You say you've been widowed for six years.' Simon thought that this was a bit bold of him, but Carolyn didn't seem to mind.

'I do have a lover, but he does not love me. He's married to someone else, and I don't see him often enough. However he is an absolutely charismatic and fascinating man and don't waste your energy telling me not to be so foolish.'

Simon, who had been about to do just that, felt put in his place for the second time that day. 'I wouldn't dream of it,' he lied. 'It must have been a hell of a blow to lose John so suddenly.'

'It knocked me sideways. But a lot of people came into my life to help me through it. In a funny sort of a way Piers was one of them. Although he is never around enough to really give support.'

'Yes,' Simon agreed. 'He likes to grace you with his presence occasionally, stir up a lot of dust, and then fly off to do the same elsewhere, leaving you to sort things out somehow. I think he gets bored with people very quickly. He is so accustomed to the fast lane and constant stimulation and change that he can't take his foot off the accelerator.'

'His health is appalling,' said Carolyn. 'Jetting around the world has destroyed his ability to sleep properly. He will be our first trial candidate for the jet lag cure. Time Warp is probably the reason he ended up backing your decision to buy Zeus so soon after Delster.'

Simon laughed. 'That's an interesting thought. But no, I've never known Piers to make a decision about anything that wasn't thought through from a business perspective. I don't think he ever wastes his time thinking about anything other than business and finance.'

'Come on, you just don't know him that well. He does have other interests you know—' Carolyn was just about to list them when Simon interrupted.

'Well whatever they are, or whoever they are, they're preventing him from coming over next week. So it looks like I've been saved from my periodic beating up.'

'Yes, I picked up a voicemail this morning from him with the news. Apparently a combination of ill health and other pressures made him decide to give the March visit a miss. Andecis is trying to buy a small company in the USA and the deal is going pear-shaped. Piers is staying put to see if he can rescue it. He says he'll be over in May for a "long" visit. I suppose "long" means a whole week instead of two or three days. He's bringing his wife with him – apparently she wants to empty the shops in Bond Street.'

'Well, that gives me a couple more months' breathing space.'

'I'm sure you could use it. For me it's rather annoying. He'd been planning to arrive on the weekend and I have two tickets for the Francis Bacon exhibition at the Tate Modern on Sunday, and a table booked at The Ivy on Sunday night. I hate Francis Bacon, but it would have been fun to laugh at his grotesque paintings with Piers.'

Simon suddenly had a vision of Carolyn, the widow, and casual lover of a married man, facing a lonely weekend on her own, let down by someone she saw as a friend. Piers was not big on empathy; he would not be able to imagine the disappointment.

'Carolyn, can I come and laugh at Francis Bacon with you?'

'Would you like to? That would be terrific. If you laugh loudly enough I'll let you take me to dinner at The Ivy as well.'

'It's a date.'

This is one for the boys, thought Simon. Here I am, going on a second date with an attractive green-eyed blonde, and it's about friendship, not sex. Yet I know we'll have a good time together and I'm already looking forward to it. The anticipation doesn't make my toes curl, but somehow it lifts my spirits.

Chapter Nine

The next few months were the most fulfilling of Simon's life so far. Angela helped him to think through a corporate strategy based on his mission. It went something like this:

- To provide top-quality drugs with a particular emphasis on improving quality of life for the older members of society.
- To grow organically and by acquisition to a position where we supply two per cent of the market.
- To create a learning organisation in which people are empowered to create and constantly improve both drugs and systems.
- To market drugs by providing support, information and education on quality of life issues to the customers.

Initially he wooed the financial press with his vision and purpose, then kept them informed as he and Roger worked through their plans for transforming the leadership and performance of the company to enable it to realise the vision. The share price stopped falling and remained steady, giving Simon some breathing space and keeping Piers off his back. Angela helped Simon to work through a broad leadership development strategy, including cultural integration. Roger joined them for a few meetings, and between them they created an expensive but comprehensive programme.

Simon, as planned, started with presenting the mission to the board and asking for their support, and for their ideas for taking it forward within their own functions, as Carolyn had done. Carolyn backed him by showing how her marketing plans supported the mission. Roger then spelt out the leadership development plans. The theme was: lead with vision and direction, coach and empower teams to achieve the operating goals implied by the vision, and delegate everything appropriate.

The leadership development programme was to include workshops, team building and individual coaching for everyone on the board and at the next level down. Coaching would also be extended to some key players at middle management level. The idea was to spell out the principles of transformational leadership in the workshops, and to use the coaches to support senior management in applying these principles in their day to day life.

'You can't suddenly change the management style in a big company without helping people to learn how to apply it in practice,' Simon explained to his board. 'The coaches will also teach us how to coach our direct reports in the most practical way possible, by giving to us what we should be giving to them, support and mentoring.'

The response to the mission was enthusiastic; board members happily went away to follow Carolyn's example with their own teams. However, when they heard Roger's leadership development plans, there was a mixed reaction.

'It's what this company has been needing for a long time.'

'Going on courses is for junior managers, isn't this a bit like teaching old dogs new tricks?'

'I've been involved with these big management development programmes before at other companies. You get a high for a while and then it fizzles and you're back at square one, but minus a lot of money.'

Simon, Roger and Carolyn patiently dealt with the concerns. But the breakthrough came when Simon made his final remarks. 'I'd like you all to know that I already have a coach, and find her a very good sounding board, and a great support. I don't think I could apply these transformational principles myself without her help. Carolyn also has a coach, and Roger is about to start with one.

'The final piece in the jigsaw is that we're going to start the programme with an in-depth assessment of the board, and the next level down. This will identify what we each need to develop and learn in order to take the company forward to achieve its vision, and strategic goals. It will also identify gaps in our armoury, and we'll recruit to fill those gaps. We're leaving nothing to chance. We all have a choice right now.

Either you throw yourselves enthusiastically into this, and use the opportunity to develop the competencies you need, · or if you haven't got the stomach for it tell us now. That goes for me as well.' Simon did not say what would happen to those without the stomach for it but he knew they would draw the right conclusions.

At their next session Angela and Simon discussed his experiences with winning the hearts and minds of his colleagues. 'You're getting the standard response,' explained Angela. 'With any big change programme people fall into three groups. First you have the trailblazers, who are energised by the whole thing. They will lead from the front with you, and support and enrich your programme from the start. Without them you'd go nowhere. Then you have the solid middle ground. They'll go along with it, partly out of loyalty and partly because it looks like the key people are behind it. If encouraged and assisted they'll give the programme their invaluable support. Finally you have the laggards. These are those people who cling to the past and think that there's nothing new to learn. The best of these will finally come on board when it is obvious that the change is going to be successful. The worst will leave, or have to be fired.'

'It all sounds rather challenging,' said Simon.

'The biggest challenge for you will be to lose your command and control habits, and to start delegating those operating details you had time to worry about when the company was half its present size.'

Simon laughed. 'I have a clear mission now, and I am completely committed to taking it forward. The universe has already sent me you, Carolyn and Roger. I have every confidence it will also send me the intelligence to learn what I have to learn. By the way, Angela, I must tell you that I'm getting friendlier with both Carolyn and Roger and it's making a difference to my life, especially my relationship with Carolyn.'

'I'm glad about that,' said Angela. 'Does that mean that Carolyn is your girlfriend?'

'No, not at all. Chance would be a fine thing. She's really just a friend. She has a lover, in fact, a married man.'

'Having a few good friends is just what the doctor ordered.'

*

Simon toured the UK and continental Europe with his message. He answered questions, dealt with challenges and performed like a star. Every time a disagreement threatened his equilibrium he harked back mentally to his mission. 'I'm here on earth to make this dream of mine come true. I want to contribute to the welfare of the ageing population, and to strengthen this company so that we can all pull together to make that contribution. The universe will give me all that I need to achieve this. I don't need to feel fear or anxiety.' Sometimes when caught by surprise by a nasty attack or unexpected bad news he used a phrase he learnt from Angela: 'I can see peace instead of this.' It worked well to calm him.

Under tuition from Angela, Roger and Carolyn, Simon began to really understand that it wasn't up to him alone to transform the company. He began to expect and get support from many quarters, not just from ghostly figures floating out there in the subatomic world but from flesh and blood people in Andecis.

As he shared his vision with the senior team, and responded to their suggestions for improving it and making it work, he was surprised by the way many of them took responsibility for transmitting it downwards and outwards. On his tour he got the local directors to present with him; he did his best to leave them with a clear and public authority for taking things forward, and he resisted hogging the lime-light. The petty squabbling caused by the integration eased off, but didn't stop. But even some of the squabblers wrote to him with suggestions for making the mission message even more compelling.

While Simon was presenting with Mike Simmons, the sales director, they had an opportunity to discuss Eric Mendez over a beer in a pub on the Avon, just outside Bristol. It was a warm day in May, so they sat outside on the pub's lawns, and watched the river gurgling past. Although it was a peaceful scene Mike seemed anything but. His restlessness showed itself in the constant readjustment of his long legs.

'This is what makes life in England such a joy,' said Simon, leaning back in his chair and savouring the long summer evening and the fresh green leaves on the trees.

'I wish I could share your peacefulness,' said Mike. 'Eric is torturing me. He has raised morale off the floor in the sales department, but he continues to make the most hair-raising decisions. Have you heard the latest?'

'No. I get the feeling that I'm not going to enjoy this,' Simon said, reluctant to let go of his pleasure in the moment.

'Recently an opinion leader, a German oncologist of considerable stature in Europe, was invited by someone in the medical department to present the results of his research on the efficacy of one of our drugs. When Eric discovered that this oncologist's findings were negative, he decided that he shouldn't be allowed to make his presentation at this prestigious international conference. To make matters worse Eric didn't involve the medical department, but dispatched a junior member of his department to break the news.'

Simon responded thoughtfully. 'Two mistakes in one. We have no tradition of throttling independent research findings, even if they do cast a poor light on drug efficacy. Secondly we don't send a boy to do a man's job.'

'The oncologist is outraged, and it will be very hard to continue what has previously been a very valuable relationship with him. When I challenged Eric he said the man was pompous and arrogant, and that we shouldn't be dealing with him anyway. My real fear is that yet another bad publicity storm is brewing.'

'It sounds as if Eric is simply not learning.'

'He's not. I think it's time to give up on him.'

'I know I suggested you sack him when we last spoke, but maybe now it's my turn to hesitate about letting him go,' Simon said, remembering the chances Piers had given him. 'I hear good things of him as well as bad. Why don't we wait until he's been through the assessments and the leadership programme? Maybe we should also give him a coach. Let's see if we can help him to move forward, and then make our decision later this year.'

'OK, if you say so. I'll try to stand it for a while longer. But I keep holding my breath and waiting for the next gaffe.'

Simon thought about Piers and wondered if that was how he felt about him. Then he remembered Angela's remarks the first time he heard her speak. 'If we see a world we dislike, full of incompetence, danger and deviousness, then that's how our world will be, we will attract these people into our lives.' Maybe there's a lesson here for Mike and for me, not just for Piers, Simon concluded.

'Mike, try to give Eric as much support and encouragement as you can, and focus on his achievements. Sometimes it happens that if we have expectations of failure for our people they then fulfil them. Bear that in mind, won't you?'

Mike looked slightly mystified but agreed to do this.

The IT department continued to wallow in a culture of slippage, never meeting deadlines or staying within budget. Simon had a meeting with Doug Allen, and his boss Andy Barton. Andy and Simon empathised with Doug over the problems he was facing and the demoralising impact of the constant complaints from internal customers. They then explained the strategic importance to Andecis of getting the systems integrated so that the drugs they were trying to bring to the market could get there.

Doug tried to explain the problems he was facing, but he lost Simon after a while. What Simon did understand was that Doug was aiming at a very technically advanced solution to the integration problem, and that it was proving impossible to do it in the time he had originally hoped. When the systems were eventually installed and running they would put them in the lead in the pharmaceutical world. The merger had forced a change anyway, so this was a golden opportunity to do something revolutionary.

Doug seemed to understand the gravity of the immediate problem, and said that he had been tearing his hair out over it. The outcome of the discussion was promising; he and Andy agreed to meet again the next day and to thrash out a short-term technical compromise that could enable the Time Warp, Eveready and Rondina projects to hit their deadlines.

Simon himself took the good news to David Jones, leader of the Rondina project. He knew he should leave it to the director of research, but he decided that he was due for a follow-up meeting with David anyway, so he went against his new principles on this occasion. Simon was very encouraged by the meeting.

'I'm impressed by what has been coming down from the board lately,' David told him. 'It looks as if we're getting some real leadership at last. The news about IT support just adds to my optimism. The workshops and coaching sound like a good strategy for developing leadership around here, and getting some consistency from the top team after the merger. I was impatient in the past because I had no confidence that things would change. Now I do. In fact my whole team feels that they're contributing to the core of what this company is all about, and that you consider them to be important. We've had the extra resources we asked for, and now we may even get a short-term IT solution. Three cheers! I don't know what the other teams think about things, especially those not working on blockbuster drugs. But I can say that my team are all behind you.'

'That's great, David.'

'I'd like to put my name in the hat for the coaching I hear is going to be made available for key players at middle-management level. You may think this is a touch arrogant, but if I don't ask I may never get the chance. The difference it's made to you is noticeable. I'd like some of that for myself.'

This was very encouraging feedback for Simon. He made a mental note to organise a coach for David and to ask the coach to teach him to be a bit less abrasive with his feedback to top management. David could go far, and a little polish and political sophistication would help him along even more. He also made a note to work with the director of research on another message, for the teams labouring away on less high-profile drugs, or on projects where the drugs were unlikely to make it to the market.

Simon returned to London after a particularly demanding week of meetings and travel. He went straight to the Mirabelle where he had arranged to meet Angela for dinner as he hadn't been able to make the coaching session planned for mid-afternoon. She had cheerfully agreed to give up her Friday evening so she could hear how things were going. 'This is far better than cooking dinner for six hungry people,' she said when Simon apologised for messing up the start to her weekend.

'Do you know, Angela,' he said, 'I do think I'm changing, or in your jargon, transforming. I feel as if I've gone through a gate which has locked shut behind me, and won't allow me back to the place I've come from. I know I have a long way to go, but I'm so excited and energised by pursuing my mission that I can't imagine going back to a "me me me" view of life.'

'I'm sure you won't go back, Simon, not if you find it so rewarding. Although you *will* have valleys sometimes. Even people with a mission don't spend their whole life on a mountain top. Oh my goodness!' This cry was a response to the enormous plate of ornately displayed sea bass and vegetables that had just been put in front of Angela. Simon looked at his fillet steak and sautéd potatoes and asked himself why women always made him feel guilty by choosing such healthy meals.

'You're probably right, but it's as if I am on a high plateau right now, and the rift valley is not in sight, only little hollows.'

'Describe to me how you're feeling, what's it like on that high plateau?'

'I am totally engaged in what I'm doing, all of my activities are gratifying and purposeful. I even put up cheerfully with travelling, traffic jams, delayed trains, hundreds of e-mails and all of the tedious things in life. I do this because there's a purpose in my life. It's not just the end customer I hope to help, but the people working in the company. I'm sure my message doesn't affect everyone in the same way, but I do feel now that I can help some people to grow, feel empowered and enjoy their working lives more. I'm just at the start of that journey, but it's great to have that as a goal. So I am pretty buoyant. I'm physically tired tonight, but I'm not tired within.'

'You have a heavy schedule, but you don't seem stressed.'

'I'm not. Suddenly I'm doing what I love. I'm no longer working just for money, but I'm doing something that makes my heart sing and that brings benefits to other people.'

'Let's drink to that,' said Angela, clinking her wine glass against his. 'I'm absolutely overjoyed for you, and what's more I can't think of anything else to say; you've said it all.'

'I've one more thing to add, and that is thank you for getting me going on this mission stuff, it's made a great difference to me. I suspect it'll change the company too, but it's early days yet.'

Simon's personal life was also going well. Edward had enjoyed the rugby match at Twickenham, especially as England won. Simon was able to entice him back into his life with other similar treats. Football, tennis and cricket as the summer got going all lured Edward up to London to see his dad. Simon was also careful to follow scrupulously the instructions for personal security from Inspector Larkman.

He could not take a risk with Edward being killed or maimed by Red Roger.

Katy had made a superb hostess at his 'coming out' party in March. Sabine Duprey, the party organiser, had been very professional, despite Simon's previous sexual rejection of her, and the party had been a great success. It also achieved its objectives in that Simon was reintegrated into a London social scene. In fact as a single eligible male he had more invitations than he could cope with. Katy was busy with her A levels, so he had not seen much of her since the summer term started.

Simon's relationship with Carolyn was blossoming. They had numerous interests in common: the opera, the theatre, art and hiking. Carolyn was a breath of fresh air with her intelligence, self-sufficiency and sense of fun. It was also a relief not to have her chasing him, unlike most of the rather desperate single or divorced women in his new social set. The divorce with Emily was finalised, and Simon felt as if the world was his oyster.

Just as he was beginning to think that it would all be plain sailing for the rest of his life, and that fear was a thing of the past, Piers arrived for the May board meeting in a thoroughly bad mood. Simon suspected that he had not spent a whole week with his wife in years. The strain was noticeable by the time of the Wednesday meeting.

'The thing is, she's a very charming and interesting woman,' Simon said to Roger on the morning of the meeting. 'But Piers cannot stand spending more than a couple of days with any human being, or on any one activity. Have you ever known him to go on holiday for more than a few days?'

'I'm not sure if I can remember him ever going on holiday.'

Carolyn had taken to her bed with the flu. 'Where is Carolyn?' was the first grumpy question from Piers as the meeting started. 'Flu! She's never ill. You guys must be putting her under too much pressure with your mad schemes for doubling the world's population by making people live twice as long.'

'Uh, oh,' said Roger *sotto voce* to Simon. 'Shades of "not invented here".'

And Carolyn is not here to make him behave. We're in for trouble, thought Simon.

They were. 'I cannot believe these figures,' shouted Piers.

'Simon, were you born stupid or have you just grown that way? Here you are, spending this fortune on training, all for a bunch of guys who'll have retired or left in the next five to ten years. Why, if you have to spend this sort of money, don't you use it to get those damn drugs to the market?'

There was silence in the room. No one made eye contact. This was the norm when Piers let fly with his temper. No one wanted to put themselves in the firing line. Much to his disappointment Simon suffered his usual negative reaction to being under attack from Piers. He felt his energy drain away, and anxiety welled up in his throat, along with anger. He kept saying to himself: I can see peace instead of this, but it didn't work. He said nothing out loud. It was so unfair after all the effort and progress of the last few months to have the whole programme threatened by Piers in a temper. The assessments were already under way, and the workshops were due to start in a few weeks. Simon became aware that his armpits were damp with sweat.

Then to everyone's surprise Peter, the financial director, cleared his throat and spoke. 'Actually Piers, there's money in the kitty for this. The financial analysts have reacted very favourably to our plans, despite their cost, and the share price has been holding steady for months . . .' His voice faded as Piers glowered at him, but before he could demolish Peter with cruel words, Roger spoke up.

'I know that the leadership development plans are largely mine, so you may not see me as entirely objective. But I must mention that the atmosphere in the company over here has been very positive since we announced our plans. Staff turnover has fallen away to well below the average for the industry. That on its own will offset some of the costs of the programme.'

Verity Roberts, the director of research, who was David Jones's boss, said: 'A miracle has happened on the Rondina team. They're all behind Simon, and David Jones has given him and the whole board a vote of confidence.'

Andy Barton was the last to join in. 'The IT department is at last starting to play ball and it looks as if they are going to be able to sellotape some things together temporarily to enable the important drug projects to hit their regulatory deadlines.'

Just as Piers opened his mouth to attack Andy over his

unfortunate terminology, Simon found his voice. 'What has happened, Piers, is that we have bought time by sharing our vision and plans. Our people feel that they are getting some much-needed leadership, and are glad to have meaningful goals to work for. If we pull back now that will soon turn into cynicism, and we will be even worse off than we were before.'

'OK, OK, you win this round, but make sure that it works. You're a great buyer of time and spender of money, Simon. I want to see some returns by the end of the year.'

Simon had to make do with that. He got no praise, no support and no approval from Piers, just suspicion and criticism. However he was delighted with the support he received from the other board members. So this is what happens when you have a team pulling together to achieve a vision. They find the courage to stand up to Piers to defend their goals. That thought comforted him as they moved on to a less contentious item on the agenda.

Later that evening Simon drove home and parked his car in the driveway of his house. As he walked up the steps to the front door he thought he saw a shadowy figure slip past his car and out into the street. There was no sign of anyone, not even of the policeman who was often to be seen outside his house these days, as part of the security arrangements to protect him from Red Roger. He decided it must be his imagination. That's the effect that Piers has on me, he thought to himself as he retraced his steps towards his front door. I'm seeing things that aren't there.

Simon went to see Carolyn in her office the following week. 'We really missed you last week at the board meeting. So, obviously, did Piers. He was in such a mood all week, he nearly made us scrap the leadership programme.'

'So I heard,' she said. 'I'm so sorry to have deserted you. I was as sick as a dog. By the time I dragged myself back to work on Friday he'd found some excuse to fly off to Tokyo and had gone, leaving his poor wife to carry her shopping home alone.'

'How are you now anyway?' asked Simon. 'You don't seem to be your usual chirpy self. You look pale. Maybe you need a holiday.'

'Yes, I've been thinking of doing some hiking in the Brecon Beacons. Why don't you come with me? I know a wonderful country house hotel right at the foot of the Black Mountains.'

'Doesn't it rain all the time there?' Simon was quite thrilled at the invitation, but tried desperately hard to be cool.

'Come on, we're hardy, intrepid English people. What's a little rain?' Simon decided to ignore the fact that Carolyn had called him English.

And so they agreed to go to Wales, setting in motion a train of events which were to have the most significant consequences for both of them.

Chapter Ten

Simon poured his heart out to Angela about his problem with Piers. He told her how he'd been overcome by negative feelings in the last board meeting when finding himself under attack yet again. 'I had been doing very well emotionally up to that point,' he said. 'Things have been going well for me, and I've been on a bit of a high. I'm encouraged by the progress we're making with our mission.'

Angela noticed that 'my' had now changed to 'our' mission.

Simon continued. 'I've experienced setbacks, but I'm pretty confident of overcoming them. We still have problems with two of our major new drugs, but I feel quietly hopeful that we'll find a way through. People have attacked me over these drug programmes, and over the spend on the leadership programme too. Normally I react badly to aggression, non-constructive criticism and defensiveness, but during the last few months I've been amazed at my ability to deal with these things. On occasion I felt angry, or slightly anxious, but recovered quickly, and found it easy to get into constructive debate without taking it personally. In fact I told you that evening we ate at the Mirabelle that I felt I was on a high plateau.

'I've developed a deep faith in the support that the universe gives to a worthwhile mission, and in my ability to create the reality I want. The immediate world I live in is now different. It is less frightening and hostile, more optimistic and has more friends in it.

'However this new-found ability of mine to create my own reality doesn't extend to Piers. He remains dominating, volatile and scary. To use your metaphor he sent me tumbling down into one of those valleys you warned me about. If my colleagues hadn't spoken up to defend the leadership project, and reinjected me with my own faith and enthusiasm, I would have bombed out. I don't want that ever to happen again.'

'What sort of relationship would you like to have with Piers?'

'I would like to be his executioner.'

Angela chuckled. 'Quite understandable, but I think you can do better than that. What would a good relationship between the two of you look like?'

'It would be one where there's mutual respect, where we listen to and acknowledge each other's points, and have constructive debate over differences of opinion. It should also include acknowledging each other's strengths and achievements.'

'You know the law of the universe: what you want you first of all give with love, then you get back tenfold.'

'I must admit that I mostly don't give Piers the things I want from him. I listen, and grudgingly admire his business acumen and good brain, but I tend to focus on his negative qualities and I definitely don't respect him. Angela, I can make an effort to be more positive in my thoughts about him, and I can envisage a more productive working relationship. I will do that. But as a strategy for solving this problem it's like using nail scissors to cut open a coconut. It's not enough.'

'I agree, but it is a start. Without that attitude, other strategies probably wouldn't work.'

'Why do you think Piers is so volatile, and why do I react so badly?'

'Now I'm going to have to give you another one of my lectures to explain it all.'

'Great, I love your lectures.' Simon sat back in his chair and looked expectantly at Angela. She was bathed in the light streaming in through her office window. Her long legs were elegantly crossed. Her black hair shone glossily in the sunlight. She has such a good effect on me, thought Simon. She is both calming and energising at the same time – just the opposite to Piers.

'Fear is at the base of it all. You and Piers are engaged in what I call a control drama which was brilliantly described by

James Redfield in his book *The Celestine Prophecy*. A control drama is a manipulative technique we learn as little children. I'll tell you about the different control dramas in a minute, but each one is a method for controlling energy. Control dramas are rooted in the original fear that if we lose the love and protection of our parents we won't be able to survive. As children, when our parents really were our source of survival, and when we needed energy to feel secure, we used a drama that seemed to work in our particular family.

'When we are this young and this vulnerable, we develop a belief that to get the energy we need in the form of approval, recognition, support, we must get it from other people. We therefore adopt a way to pull these forms of energy in our direction by the control dramas we learn in our families. It's a way of defending ourselves against that awful feeling when energy drains out of you as a result of some withering put-down, threat, abuse, neglect, guilt and so forth.'

'That's a very familiar feeling. I can remember something very similar with my father and later on with Emily.'

'Unfortunately when someone like Piers or Emily manipulates your energy or attention the strong negative emotions stop you from listening to your intuition. You then lose the inner guidance that would have helped you to make a better decision and do something positive.'

'I can believe it. When Piers attacked me in public my energy drained away. It came back when my team supported me, and only then was I able to find something mature and positive to say.'

'Control dramas are powerful manipulative techniques, but they are largely played out at an unconscious level.'

'Tell me about these control dramas then,' said Simon. 'I want to make sure I learn how to use them properly.'

Angela threw back her head and laughed. 'That's hardly the point. I'm going to tell you about them in an effort to help you to stop using them!'

'Oh!' Simon felt rather foolish.

'James Redfield identified four control dramas. The intimidator, the interrogator, the poor me and the aloof. The intimidator gets attention and thereby energy through threats, put-downs, sarcasm, domineering behaviour and unexpected outbursts. These are all behaviours designed to make the other person feel afraid or anxious. The intimidator creates an aura of negative power and sucks energy away from you towards him or her.'

'That sounds familiar.'

'The interrogator is less threatening but breaks down your spirit and will by questioning everything you do or say. They are hostile critics who look for ways to make you wrong. As you strive to defend or prove yourself your energy drains away and goes towards them.

'The aloof person uses behaviour that ranges from disinterested, unavailable, uncooperative to condescending, rejecting, contrary and sneaky. They believe unconsciously that if they appear mysterious or detached others will come to draw them out. They gain attention, initially, through their mysterious, hard-to-get persona. As people do seek them out or try to make them commit, they get a surge of energy.

'The poor me or victim doesn't feel they have enough power to confront the world in an active way. So they elicit sympathy, and get energy by manipulating others into helping or looking after them. They initially seduce by their vulnerability and need for help. But they're not really interested in solutions because they would lose their source of energy.'

'I do all of those, at times.'

'So do I,' said Angela. 'But I have my favourites.'

'I can't imagine you needing to get energy by manipulating it out of other people,' said Simon in surprise.

'Well, it's true that I've lost the need to use these much, but, like you, I'm still capable of getting caught out at times. Which are your favourites?'

'Aloof is probably my most frequent drama. It's certainly the drama I get hooked into by Piers. I use intimidator and interrogator when someone who is being incompetent or lazy threatens a goal of mine. I don't think that I use poor me that often.'

'The dramas tend to match each other. When you use intimidator you often get people manipulating you with poor me in self-defence. They try to stop you in your tracks by making you feel guilty. On the other hand intimidator behaviour may attract counter-intimidator behaviour in aggressive personalities. Occasionally an intimidator attracts aloof behaviour.

'Interrogators often attract aloof dramas and sometimes

poor me's. Both of these are attempts to escape the probes. Aloofs use their dramas to escape having to answer the hostile questions and attempts to prove them wrong which of course drains their energy.'

'That's it. I go into aloof to prevent all of my energy drain-ing away when Piers is trying to make me roll in dirt. It doesn't work very well, but it's all I've got. It is a lifelong pattern. As a child I would go and lock myself in my bedroom when my father had given me a verbal beating in the vain hope that he would come up to my bedroom and lure me back into the bosom of the family and say he was sorry. He never came, but my mother would sometimes and that was better than nothing. Now I use it with Piers and it doesn't work with him either. He never apologises, never, however outrageous he has been.' Simon gave in to a wave of self-pity. He wondered why he had such crosses to bear.

'Why do you think Piers uses interrogator or intimidator with you?'

'I suppose like any other high achiever he is driven by fear of failure when he sees something possibly going wrong. Then he loses control and lets you have it. He has a huge appetite for control, he needs to know everything.'

'Why don't you tell him everything?'

'I suppose there are two answers to that. The obvious answer is because as soon as you tell him something he wants to take over and tell you how to do it or do it himself. I could deal with that if I had a way of holding on to my wits and my self-esteem. I do stand up for myself occasionally over things that really matter, like the leadership development programme, and he sometimes gives ground. The answer that wasn't so obvious until today is that we are both involved in this unconscious, childish control drama, in-terrogator or intimidator versus aloof.'

'That's right. You're both caught up in a horrendous dance, called the low-energy shuffle.'

'Yes! He is a Dementor and I'm Harry Potter!'

'What do you want to do about it?'

'I knew you would get round to asking that eventually. I want to end it, but I don't know how to disengage. I can't change his behaviour. It's a strong habit. He uses intimidator once or twice a day with someone, not just with me. Interestingly, in between he is energetic, charming and witty.

He would be great company and a good mentor if you were not on tenterhooks waiting for the next outburst, the next fall from grace.'

Simon looked at his watch.

'Do you need to go?'

'I do really but I'll stay a bit longer. I'd like to get to the bottom of this.'

'More coffee?'

Simon nodded and Angela poured him a cup from the flask on the table. He gulped down the coffee, needing the boost to counter the draining emotions caused by reliving scenes with Piers and his father.

'The trouble with getting hooked into a control drama, as you are with Piers, is that the gains are short-term. Eventually it becomes counterproductive, it's bad for both of you. The energy you gain from putting someone down, or by withdrawing into aloof, doesn't last very long. You may feel more powerful for a short while, but the other person is left weakened, and will often fight back. For example Piers finds other ways to get the information you withhold from him, then he goes on the attack. Accept for the moment that you can't change his behaviour. Can you change your own?'

'I guess I have changed it quite a lot lately. I don't use the control dramas anything like as much as I used to.'

'I suspect you've been able to change because you no longer see the only source of energy as being outside of you, in the people in your life. You now understand that the universe is benign and loving and sends you energy to help you to achieve your dreams. Once you remember that you create your own reality and have the power to alter things for the better so that you realise your mission, there's much less need to feel fear. You don't need to control the people around you to get energy. That's when you drop your manipulative techniques.'

'You're right, of course. But somehow I can't help wishing Piers would drop dead.'

Angela smiled sympathetically and brushed her black hair away from her eyes. 'That would be a shame. He's a gift to you. He is in your life right now, pulled in by you, by your loving unconscious, seeking to give you another chance to end the pattern of aloof dramas you started as a child. Even if Piers died, as your father did, the problem would not be solved. Until you lick the dramas yourself your unconscious will obligingly continue to attract interrogators into your life for you. So you might as well have a go at sorting this out now. Try to be more interested in what's causing you to be judgemental, rather than thinking about what's 'wrong' with Piers. After a while you might find that you can replace judgement with a gentle inward look at what is hooking you.'

'I'm sure that you're right about that aloof, interrogator drama being the hook, although I'm not quite sure at this point how easy it's going to be to get unhooked.'

'The two factors that most inhibit our personal transformation are negativity and judgement. What bothers us most about others are things that we refuse to acknowledge in ourselves, or something we need more of. Just keep the focus on yourself, your hooks, and your growth needs, and away from judgement of Piers. You'll find that it helps.'

'I'll just have to pray for help because I don't know where to go from here. It's frustrating to see your own dysfunctional behaviour and not know what to do about it.'

'Prayer will certainly help. Just think, the universe is doing everything it can to help you to remove this control drama from your repertoire of behaviours. It sent you your father, then Piers, then me to help you to see it more clearly. Surely such a helpful universe will also help you to find the answer if you ask it.'

Simon sat forward in his chair, energy flooding back into him. 'That has helped me to get back in touch with my faith in finding a way forward.'

'I do also have a more immediately practical suggestion.' Angela too leant forward and smiled her sweet smile again. 'Can you do anything to reduce Piers's fears, and so reduce his need to use intimidator and interrogator with you?'

'Only what you challenged me on, which is to give him the information he always wants, and which I withhold from him as much as possible.'

'It'll take time to work, but it sounds like a sensible idea. Once he has enough information to feel more in control of the show in Europe, he'll use interrogator less with you. Your energy will remain higher, and you won't have your back against the wall all the time. Also, remember to focus on your contribution and your mission when you're with him. Use that focus to replace thoughts about what you're getting, or losing. Try to send him your energy instead of fear and low respect. Remember, thoughts are a powerful part of our universe and they alter reality.

'When we use our thoughts to send positive energy we avoid competing for energy. We uplift the other person and he or she will use this energy to be more positive towards you. They'll lose the need to manipulate.'

'Let me summarise this new strategy for managing my relationship with Piers,' Simon said. 'I'll use my imagination to visualise more positive interactions with him, and I'll give him the respect and acknowledgement I want from him. I'll look for ways to reduce his fear so that he feels less need to use control dramas with me. I'll do this by inundating him with all the information he could possibly want. I'll remember to focus on the mission, the universal energy that's helping me to achieve it, and my desire to give rather than get. Finally I'll send appreciative thoughts towards him, to raise his energy. And I'll keep praying for help. I really want to crack this. Actually, Angela, seeing Piers as a gift sent to help me with personal growth is quite an insight. I feel better towards him already.'

They both sat in thoughtful silence for a while, and then Simon spoke again.

'It's funny, you know. Carolyn seems to understand Piers, she sees right through his gruff exterior, and focuses on the good things about him. So she doesn't feel frightened or manipulated by him. And now you seem to see him in the same light.'

'It's not that I don't think he's a bully. But I'm trying to help you to see that you have the power to change your response to him, and perhaps to change his behaviour towards you.'

'Yes, that's sinking in. This has been very useful, Angela. I'll see you in a few weeks' time.'

When Simon left Angela had an insight as she typed up the meeting notes. I bet that married lover of Carolyn's that Simon told me about a few weeks ago is Piers, she thought. I feel it in my bones. When Simon finds out it'll send him right back to square one. Isn't it sad how you often fail to see something that's right under your nose.

Chapter Eleven

Simon and Carolyn managed to take their holiday in the Brecon Beacons in early June. 'We got away just in time,' said Carolyn happily as they cruised along the motorway in Simon's big Mercedes. 'A month later and the Black Mountains will be swarming with schoolchildren on holiday, not to mention their parents. I'm very crowd-averse, especially in the countryside.'

She was even happier when they rolled up at the Pennyrest Hotel, a thirteenth-century farmhouse, just north of Abergavenny. The owners, Roy and Julia, rushed out to greet her like a long-lost friend. The hotel looked like something out of a fairytale, with crooked walls and chimneys, and creaky floors. It was beautifully restored, with great attention to historical detail. They discovered that the floors in their bedrooms were on a slope.

'If I get up in the night to go to the loo I'll be able to roll back to bed,' said Simon. Carolyn was ecstatic about her bathroom, which was huge, with a very old, but probably not thirteenth-century, bathtub in the middle of the room. They behaved like children, exploring a new playground.

'I hope you don't frighten me by trying to sneak into my bed in the middle of the night,' said Simon, noticing that there was no sexual tension between them and rather wishing that there were.

'I'll try to restrain myself.'

'Well, there's no need to try too hard.'

'Right,' said Carolyn, adopting a jolly-hockey-sticks manner. 'Let's put on our walking boots and head for the mountains.'

They got lost looking for Offa's Dyke and ended up driving

for miles up and down narrow country lanes. 'I'm not sure if we brought the best vehicle for this expedition,' said Simon, struggling to turn the car to correct a wrong turn down an impossibly narrow lane. Carolyn seemed to find the whole thing rather funny, so he stayed in a good mood. Eventually, just as they were about to give up, they saw a signpost to Offa's Dyke, conveniently at a place where the road widened enough for them to park on the verge. They left the car at a precarious angle, half expecting to find it had somersaulted down the hill when they returned.

They walked for hours over the tops of the moors along the dyke path. They looked at ruined castles, spectacular views and the rotting carcasses of dead sheep. Simon's mobile rang just as they were munching their sandwiches, but it was only Katy, wishing him a happy holiday, and giving him news of her exams. Carolyn's mood changed as the day wore on and tiredness caught up with her. She lost her childish elation and became quiet and almost broody. At dinner that night Simon asked if there was anything the matter.

'No, not really,' said Carolyn, struggling to make her way through a huge meal of roast lamb and roast potatoes. 'I'm tired and that tends to make me turn inwards. I'll make an effort to be more communicative.'

When the same thing happened the next evening Simon got anxious and asked her if it was something to do with him. 'Are you worried in case I'm contemplating an assault upon your person?' he joked, wishing that he had the audacity to do just that.

'No, Simon, that's the furthest thing from my mind. I do have something that's distracting me, but it is not anything to do with you, rest assured.'

'Is it personal or work?'

'Both, in a way.'

Simon instantly thought of Piers. 'It's Piers, isn't it?'

'Yes, I guess I just can't keep it from you. Besides, I could do with a male perspective on the problem.'

'Go on, tell me about it. I'll be your coach and your counsellor. It'll be nice to reverse roles for a change. Is your friend Piers giving you a hard time?'

'Simon. Piers is not just my friend, he's my lover.'

'What! Come to think of it I should have realised. Now that I know I can see all the clues.'

'I'm surprised you hadn't guessed. Perhaps what Piers says about deception is true after all, that the best place to hide a tree is in a forest.'

'I must take my hat off to you. If I was a woman I would never have the courage to take a lover like Piers. The very thought makes me feel rather faint and feeble. Now tell me the story, and tell me what's worrying you and I'll listen carefully and then advise you to leave him tomorrow.'

Carolyn laughed. 'I've been trying to leave him tomorrow for years. For me it takes more courage to leave him than it does to be his lover. In many ways he's a wonderful lover ...'

'Tell me how you met, and how it started. From the beginning, please.'

'Like I said before, it was six months after John died. I decided that I needed to get away from Cincinnati, and all the awful memories of John's brief illness. So I went on my own to Grand Cayman and stayed at the Hyatt. It's a fairly nice hotel, with a rather crowded beach. But the sea is so clear and blue, and the sand so white, that I fell in love with the place. I had a rather solitary retreat there until the second week, when Piers turned up. He'd come with his top team from Andecis to have a bonding session.'

'I remember hearing about that, but at that time I wasn't senior enough to be invited. I was quite envious.'

'You were right to be. They were having a wonderful time, going fishing, sailing and scuba-diving in the day, and partying at night. Piers hosted a cocktail party in the little beach restaurant called Hemingway's the first night they arrived. The men outnumbered the women, mostly personal assistants and a few local lovelies. So when I walked in by mistake, looking for an early supper, I wasn't allowed to leave. I noticed Piers across the room while I was chatting to some of his guests. He looked very attractive, and also strangely familiar, although we had never met. Eventually, I just felt compelled to go over and speak to him. The people he was with faded away soon after we began our conversation. I guess they could see the sparks flying between us. As soon as we were alone he began to chat me up. I was totally overwhelmed. I tried to play it cool, but I was lost from the start.

'He told me that he had a wife and family. I've always disapproved of adultery because of the pain it causes. Yet I never told him to go away as I should've done. The rest of the holiday was as unreal as a dream. All my hard-earned peace flew out of the window. He pursued me relentlessly whenever we were together, which was not that often as he was busy with his troops, and constantly on his mobile phone. It was very hard to have an uninterrupted conversation with him. But I still didn't tell him to go away.

'A few days after our first meeting I went jogging early in the morning. On the way back to the hotel I saw Piers running towards me, rather faster than I could manage. You know he's a marathon runner?'

'He makes me sick, he's so good at everything.' Simon tried to turn his envy into admiration, but it wasn't easy.

'Yes, he does have a way of making a person feel humble, just by being his over-talented self. Anyway he was delighted to see me, and asked me to run with him up a deserted path beside a canal. We ran together for a while, and then we walked. I surprised myself by turning to him and saying, "You know, you have completely unsettled me." He took hold of my shoulders and said, "That's the first sign you've given that you're interested in me." We kissed and that was the beginning of a relationship that has lasted, on and off, for six years.

'At first it was wonderful. He flew to Cincinnati every month partly to do business, and partly to see me. Sometimes he would invite me to New York and we would stay in his apartment overlooking Central Park. He kept his wife locked away in their home in the Hamptons. Those were magic times. I love New York City, and being there with him made it extra-special for me. We would get up at six or seven and run together in the park. In between phone calls and meetings we roamed around the city and visited galleries and museums. It was so strange to hear him shouting aggressively on the phone to someone, and to contrast that with the tenderness he showed to me. He would usually turn his mobile off just before dinner and give me his full attention, then I would melt with joy.'

'What was he like in bed?' Simon was surprised at himself for asking this, but he was too curious to leave it unasked.

'I should have realised that you'd be more interested in the sex than in the relationship. He was great, pretty relentless. If I hadn't met him before the days of Viagra I would have suspected him of taking it.'

'Trust him to be good at that as well.'

'Actually I could only cope with his sexual appetite because we were never together for more than two or three days at a time. By the end of a visit with him I was usually on my knees, happy, but slightly crippled.' Carolyn smiled ruefully.

'After a while the visits and phone calls became less frequent and I began to get the feeling he was tiring of me. This has been a recurring theme in the relationship. He can't stand more than a few days at a time of a woman's company. On the one or two occasions when I outstayed my welcome he withdrew inside of himself and I felt quite forsaken. In fact he blew hot and cold all the way through those six years. I ended the affair twice, because I felt that he was losing interest. He agreed easily, far too easily, to stop seeing me each time, and I fell into a black hole of depression. I struggled my way through these, regained my equilibrium, and then he would come back into my life. We're now in the third reincarnation of our relationship. Each time he promises that it will be better, and each time the old pattern re-establishes itself. There is intense closeness, both physical and emotional, and then he runs away. Sometimes I don't hear from him for weeks. Sometimes I don't see him for many months at a time. I just feel neglected.

'So yes, I am planning to leave him tomorrow yet again. When I say to him that I'm very low down in his priorities he says, "Yes, I have a lot of them." And I'm afraid I think that some of those priorities are other women.'

'You're right about that, Carolyn. He is clearly very fond of you, but he does have other women. He boasts of them to me occasionally, and I must tell you that the last boast was a few months ago when he stood you up for that Francis Bacon exhibition. He was crowing about how even the flu didn't dampen his ability to perform.'

Carolyn sat for a long time looking out through the window at the twilight. They were alone in the lounge of the hotel, the other guests having all gone elsewhere. Two tears trickled down her cheeks. 'I just hate having to face up to this dreadful reality, and please don't remind me that I've created it, I can't cope with that right now.'

Simon went and sat beside her on the sofa and put his arms round her. 'You're too good for him, sweetheart. Piers doesn't know how to love. I know that you are important to him, but his work is his life. He can rarely take the time to think about anything else. I'm sure that these other women don't matter all that much to him, not anything like you do. But he probably doesn't have the capacity to be committed or faithful.'

'You're right. I've always thought that he stays married so that he has the perfect excuse not to commit to anyone else. I'm throwing my love and my life away on a loner. I've come to realise this, but I do feel sad about giving him up.'

Simon lay awake for a long time that night thinking about Carolyn and Piers. He was surprised to find that mixed in with his sympathy for her was a considerable amount of jealousy. There was a joke about Piers among the New York directors of Andecis. 'If you go to a party with Piers, head for the second-best-looking woman in the room. Don't bother with the best-looking one because Piers will get her.'

I can't pretend that I don't get lovely women running after me, he thought as he drifted off to sleep in his bedroom with its creaky old floors, but they're all wacky. I think I would like a woman like Carolyn, who is beautiful inside as well as outside, and passionate to boot.

The rest of the holiday was like a good dream. They walked all over the Black Mountains, through the forests and up on to the high moors with the sheep. They sometimes walked in companionable silence, and at other times they talked. Carolyn was the sort of person you can talk to about absolutely anything, Simon realised with delight. Carolyn, finding it helpful to get her feelings about Piers off her chest, did so whenever she felt the urge. Her mood improved until she was her charming lively self again.

'I have six weeks to plan my exit speech,' said Carolyn on the last day of their holiday. All of the directors were due to go to New York in July for the Andecis senior management conference. Piers would of course be there. 'I must be careful this time to say goodbye and not au revoir. Also, I have to say it face to face, not over the phone.' They discussed ways of making the goodbye a final one this time and came up with a strategy.

'You must give him a strong disincentive to continue the relationship,' said Simon.

'That shouldn't be too difficult, I know he's terrified of anything that threatens his marriage and family life,' said Carolyn, chomping on her picnic lunch as they sat up on the tops of the moors overlooking the ruins of Llanthony Priory. The sun was shining, the sky was cobalt blue, and the Priory sat like a jewel in the greenest of fields. She felt strong after her week in the mountains, able to face life without Piers. She hadn't seen him for over four months, so presumably it wouldn't make a great deal of difference to have him completely out of her life. But they both worked for the same company now, so they would come into contact, if only at board meetings. Carolyn knew that he would keep trying to re-establish the relationship unless this ending was very final. She did not want to leave Andecis, not even to escape Piers; she was committed to the company and to the people there, and she had bought into Simon's dream.

'All I need to do is to say I don't want a casual relationship with him any more, it causes me too much pain. Either we must marry, now, or we must part. I'll put the ball in his court, ask him to decide whether he wants me enough to leave his wife, and he'll run a mile.'

'I think you're right,' said Simon, putting himself in Piers's shoes. 'Piers doesn't see much of his wife and family, but they mean a lot to him. I would never have given up my marriage if I hadn't been forced to do so. Piers won't like giving you up – after all, until now he's been able to have his cake and eat it. But he'll be threatened by a challenge like that, and will probably play it safe and stay away from you.'

'I am quietly resolved to do this,' said Carolyn. 'Simon, you have been such a help.' And she gave him a hug and a kiss, flavoured with the cheese and onion sandwich she had just eaten.

Later in the day they scrambled down the hill and had a cup of tea in the hotel beside Llanthony Priory. Carolyn was a little sad after making her big decision, but they agreed to put all thoughts of Piers aside and found no difficulty in doing so. When Carolyn went off the loo Simon gave his mother a quick call on his mobile phone to tell her about his wonderful holiday.

'We walked a hundred miles in a week,' he said after explaining to her where he was.

'What did you do that for?' she asked. 'Did you not have your car with you?' Simon sighed. Some leopards never change their spots.

They both returned to London in good spirits. Simon was happy to be back in his house again, and quite pleased to have level floors to walk on. After throwing his bags down he listened to the messages on his telephone. The first message was delivered in a strong Birmingham accent. 'This is Red Roger here. I thought you might like to know that you are now number three on the death list.'

Chapter Twelve

'Angela, I'm in a bad way.' It was the Monday afternoon immediately following Simon's holiday, and Angela had found a space for him in her schedule. This time her cheerful office and her calm gaze did not make him feel better. First he talked to her about Red Roger's message.

'I'm scared. I know we're doing all we can about security, but every time I think of it I lose trust in the benign nature of the universe. I find myself thinking that something terrible is going to happen to me, even though Inspector Larkman assures me that the security is as tight as humanly possible.'

Just as Angela was about to say something sympathetic he carried on anxiously with his tale.

'Carolyn told me while we were in Wales that Piers is her lover. That's not been good for my peace of mind either. I find myself hating the guy again. I'm disappointed in myself because I've been making such good progress until now. With your help I've become optimistic and purposeful much of the time, and I've also been getting on much better with Piers. I now communicate with him regularly, which he seems to appreciate, and I've been sending him positive vibes. This is paying off. He is noticeably less volatile and threatening with me, although he's still nervous about the money we're pouring into the IT department, and thinks we should replace Doug Allen. Until my holiday, I've been able to focus on his positive qualities. On a good day I can even see that behind his attacks, which still occur from time to time, there's a concern for my growth and performance. He is, in his heavy-handed way, trying to coach me.

'It therefore frustrates the hell out of me that I've regressed to a state where I grant him the power to push my hot buttons and make me anxious. I'm working hard on my control drama, and it helps me to have this understanding. But too often when I think of him I descend into feelings of defensiveness, inadequacy and resentment. And the Red Roger menace just compounds it.'

'I think descend is the right word,' said Angela.

'What do you mean?' asked Simon.

'What you're doing is descending into your lower self, where your ego reigns in a parallel universe of fear. All of your negative feelings come from this fear. What we experience when we're in our lower selves comes from our illusion of separateness and from forgetting that we create our own reality.'

'So I could deal with these negative emotions by reminding myself that we're all one in the universe, and not separate from each other.'

'Yes. Piers and Red Roger are both parts of you that you've pulled into your life to help you to learn your next big lesson. Don't knock yourself for being in your lower self and experiencing fear. We all do it. It is part of being human. The ego needs to be reminded of its superiority over others, in a world of scarcity, and so you find yourself in conflict. And as you admit yourself, this conflict starts in your head.

'The lower self is the bit of us that constantly searches for something out there to make our life complete. When we're in our lower selves we feel alienated, lonely and empty. No matter what we have, we never feel fulfilled. There's always something to worry about, something not right. When you listen to your lower self your experience of life makes you fearful, and you stop yourself from growing.

'Then your awareness becomes distracted from the present moment. We project the pain from the past into the future and trigger off fear based thoughts. We no longer experience just being, and the pleasure of it. Your fear and stress come from either reliving the past or fretting about possible futures like, for example, attacks from Red Roger.'

'That's exactly what's happening to me at the moment,' cried Simon. He began to hope that Angela might help him find a way out of the mire.

Angela nodded and carried on, pleased that he was listening so intently. 'When you're seduced or threatened by external circumstances you lose power and peace, and the circumstances gain power over you. Impatience is the biggest pitfall. Being impatient is a way of punishing yourself as it creates stress, dissatisfaction and fear. Also, when you work solely for money your motivation is getting rather than giving. Until you switch, as you've done, to a giving mentality, you're operating from your ego and concentrating on the things of the world, rather than love. This casts you into alien emotional territory where you're always afraid.'

'I have to confess, Angela, that I'm still inclined to see Piers and Red Roger as real threats out there, and I find it hard to control my fear and frustration.'

'You can fool yourself that the world out there creates your problems, but the source of all of your suffering is the ego that reigns in your lower self. It's the ego that makes you worry, take things personally, feel despair or resentment, and anticipate disaster. It can also make you criticise and judge others, feel hurried and driven and that life is meaningless. It's not that Piers and Red Roger aren't real, it's the way your ego makes you react to them that's the problem.

'When you're in your lower self you put out negative energy into the world, and this attracts negative experiences into your life.'

'I've thought of a way of attracting some positive experiences into our lives right now,' said Simon, looking at the bright blue sky through Angela's office window and feeling a need to lift his spirits. 'Let's have the rest of our meeting in Green Park.'

'What a superb idea.' Angela dug her sunglasses out of her handbag and they walked out of the building, looking slightly conspiratorial. Their muscles melted as soon as they were out in the warm summer sun. They walked down to St James's Palace, then wove their way through narrow streets between imposing stately stone mansions. Finally an alleyway took them past Selwyn House and into the park.

'I feel completely different out in the sunshine,' said Simon as they strolled through the park. 'Tell me, where am I when I'm feeling positive and optimistic and aware of the benign nature of the universe?'

'You're in your higher self. This is the real, wonderful you, without any of the limitations of anger, fear, jealousy, doubt, vengeance or resentment. It's a place in you where there's no

108

negativity and judgement, only unconditional love. It's a joyous and peaceful place. When you're there you're able to tap into the universal energy, and use all the wisdom and compassion available to you. This is because you no longer suffer the illusion that you're separate and alone.'

'It sounds like a great place to be.'

'You're right. It's far more enjoyable to be there than anywhere else. The higher self only wants you to be at peace. It doesn't judge, compare or demand that you defeat anyone, or be better than anyone else. It doesn't produce any of those fear-based emotions that retard your evolution. When you're in your higher self you're grateful for what you've got, rather than regretting what you lack. In this state of gratitude the universe provides abundantly. The less you need to have more, the more you get. You're never a victim. When you're in your higher self, you're always responsible for creating your own reality. You know that your mind is a projector and your life is the screen. You find yourself loving what you do, and you notice how effortlessly you achieve.'

They ducked out of the way of a crowd of happy, laughing schoolgirls who bore down on them, not looking where they were going. They're in their higher selves, thought Simon.

'The term higher self implies rising above that part of us that dwells on petty things. It's a plane of existence that has little to do with everyday upsets and struggles. You're absolutely free when you're not consumed with your own self-importance, and when you don't need to be approved of by everyone.'

Angela made these points as they walked through Green Park and crossed under the busy streets via the subway into Hyde Park. They sat on a bench in the gardens facing the arches of climbing roses and took pleasure in the colours and the smells of the flowers. A tramp limped past with a half-empty beer bottle in his hand.

'I recognise that place you've been talking about,' said Simon. 'It's a new place for me, but I feel drawn to it more and more. I'm much more effective when I'm in this higher self of mine. In fact this discussion has helped me find it again. Now I can face the Red Roger threat and put it in perspective against the thorough security measures, and the fact that past threats from animal rights groups have never materialised.' He was feeling very much better.

'You're more effective because you're not letting fear block the flow of energy from the universe towards you. You're open to receiving this universal energy, which we experience as intuitive insights and unconditional love. When you're in this state you put your best you forward, the wise loving you. You feel pulled towards it because it's where your life wants you to be. This is what you were born to do, to follow your higher self and go where it leads you. At present it's leading you towards achieving your mission with Andecis. At another stage in your life it'll lead you towards yet another compelling and fulfilling purpose.'

'How can I give myself a leg up to move into my higher self? It's not only Piers or death threats that send me tumbling into this hell. Sometimes when I'm tired, or have had a stressful day, or remember something worrying, or sad, down I go.'

'There are some steps you can take to help you to spend less time in your lower self. The ego never stops trying to pull you down. It supplies you with a large proportion of those 90,000 thoughts you have in a day, so many of which are negative. There's an exercise you can use to train your mind to focus on the positive, and to distract you from those negative thoughts, which keep you down in your lower self. I've adapted this exercise from Susan Jeffers' book, *Feel the Fear and Do It Anyway*. It goes like this. Twice a day, morning and evening answer these questions:

- What is good about right now?
- What am I looking forward to?
- What am I grateful for?

'The most important of these question is "What am I grateful for?" Gratitude disallows feelings of being separate and alienated from the universe of fellow souls, and from God. It dispels the idea that we don't have enough. It stops us from focusing on what's missing. If you practise answering these questions daily it'll eventually become easier to use them at those times when something has triggered a descent into this hell we call the lower self. You'll be able to use the questions, with their focus on the positive, to pull yourself up into your higher self.'

Simon looked at Angela, relaxed on the park bench. He took in her intelligent and beautiful blue eyes set in her calm face. Is she just professionally composed, he pondered, or is

110

that the peacefulness of her higher self that I see? I rather think it's the latter. Just then Angela remembered her sunglasses and put them on, so her eyes were hidden.

'That sounds like a good idea. I'll give it a try. Gradually I think these techniques and understandings you have given me are changing me into a more positive, purposeful person. I am at peace more of the time now. It's good and I want to stay like that as much as possible.'

'There's another trick you can use to stay in your higher self,' said Angela. 'Refuse to defend yourself to anyone. Use your inner calm to allow those who disagree with you to have their own points of view. Of course you can debate, but let go of that need to be defensive or dominating. Then you'll remain at peace.'

'I'm doing that quite a lot these days, which is probably why I'm in my higher self more often. I stand my ground over the really important issues, but I do listen more, feel less threatened by different points of view, and am much more ready to negotiate. In fact because I've changed my approach in this way I'm much more likely to agree new and more creative solutions to sticky problems. I've even done this with Piers on one or two occasions.'

'Everyone like Piers, who can still push your buttons and send you into a frenzy, or into despair, is a master teacher disguised as a difficult, volatile person. Peace means being at peace with these people, as well as with your friends. Just remember to keep seeing him as a gift.'

'I'll keep trying. I can see now that personal growth is about training and exercising your mind to see things differently, so that you will do things differently. I'm no longer deceived into thinking that you get peace of mind by changing external circumstances. It works the other way round. You change the internal first and then the external changes. It's just that when I'm in my lower self I forget about it.

'I'm on a pretty rigorous self-improvement programme,' Simon continued. 'You're helping me to train my mind, and Carolyn is getting me to train my body. She has me going jogging with her twice a week, and she keeps trying to get me to up it to three. In fact we run in Hyde Park and we often pass through these gardens. She says that if you do aerobic exercise for forty-five minutes three times a week, you seriously retard the ageing process.'

111

'She's right,' said Angela. 'She's a good influence on you. She sounds to me as much a gift you've attracted into your life as is Piers. Only the way you learn from her is much more positive and enjoyable.'

'You can say that again!'

'Coming back to Piers and the quest to improve the way you manage that relationship, I have a more practical, earthy point to make. I think that part of the reason you feel so vulnerable and fearful of Piers is because you've not done enough in Andecis to get global sponsorship and support. You're now giving real leadership and direction in Europe. Who have you got outside Europe, especially in the USA, to sponsor and champion you and your mission?'

'I haven't really thought about that. I guess I am pretty dependent on backing from Piers. You're right, that does leave me exposed if I should lose his support, such as it is.' Simon looked thoughtful.

'It strikes me that although you travel around in Europe a lot, you don't very often go further afield, and you seldom go to New York. This is a shame, as most of the powerful movers and shakers are based there, although I appreciate that Piers is the most powerful of them all. I would guess that no one in New York knows you all that well.'

'No. They'll only know what Piers has to say of me.'

'You could change that. You have an opportunity with this global senior management conference coming up in July to get to know the other big wheels. Are you speaking at the conference?'

'I have a slot. I have to report on our progress in Europe.'

'Use it well. Win them over with your mission and strategy, the leadership programme and the already noticeable results. This could be a golden opportunity for you to impress and win sponsors.'

'I'll do that. When we next meet I'll bring a draft of my speech and you can help me to knock it into shape and to rehearse it. I need to rehearse like mad to give a half-decent presentation, otherwise I get nervous and freak out. You know what they say about the human brain: it starts working the moment you're born and never stops until you stand up to speak in public.'

'Public speaking is another one of those triggers that sends a person down into their fearful lower selves. But the fates are conspiring to help you overcome this problem. Can you see how the discovery that Piers is Carolyn's lover, and the death threat, led to our conversation on methods for staying in your higher self?'

'Yes, that's an inspiring thought. Come to think of it giving a presentation from your higher self is the only way to do it without nerves. Maybe Piers and Red Roger really are gifts to me after all! I'll add these new techniques you've taught me to my preparation. Now that you've got me thinking about my feelings of vulnerability, there's something else that triggers my fear. I'd like to talk it over with you.'

'Please do.'

'OK, but first let's have an ice cream.' Simon pulled Angela to her feet and they queued up for a few minutes at the ice cream van.

'I'll have a bunny ear in mine please.'

'You can tell you've got young kids,' laughed Simon, ordering one for himself.

'Actually it's me that's the young kid.'

They walked a bit further into the park and sat on a bench beside the Serpentine. As they ate their ice creams they watched the ducks and geese waddling around on the water's edge.

'It's Doug Allen who's the other trigger for my fear,' Simon said after a while. 'Strengthening the company to achieve our mission depends so much on IT getting its act together. We have to get Time Warp through the regulators this autumn, or we'll have no new drugs for the market this year. Similarly success for Evereadiness and Rondina next year are critical for us financially. Doug now seems to understand how crucial it is to support these programmes and produce short-term solutions. He has made a case for a massive increase in full-time staff and contractors. I have to decide whether to make this investment in him, or to give up and replace him. Piers wants me to do the latter.'

'Doug has been through the assessment programme, hasn't he?' asked Angela.

'Yes. He came out with all the technical competencies, as well as the creativity needed to take us forward. He's a very clever man. But the assessment reinforced our view of him as a hopeless operational manager.'

'If you keep him he'll need a deputy to do this operational

management. Expecting him to change in that field is too much to ask, especially in so short a time.'

'That's a good point. But it adds to the scale of the investment in resources for his department. We've already poured a lot of money down that particular drain.'

'His department is critical to the success of your mission. It needs all the tender loving care you can give,' said Angela. 'If you pour more money into his department without sharing a positive vision of success with him, it could fail. If you share the positive vision, but fail to provide him with the resources he needs, then that may be another formula for failure. Doing both has to be your best bet. It's similar to a conversation I had recently with my son about passing his exams. I told him that lying on his bed and visualising success would not do the trick on its own. He was disappointed to hear that positive images only work if you accompany them with necessary action.'

Simon laughed. 'I suspect I'll need to have a similar debate with Edward. While I think about it I have another problem executive, Eric Mendez, the head of sales for Europe. He could probably do with some of your wisdom. Have you got space in your schedule for another coaching client?'

'Yes, I have space and I'd be happy to coach him. He doesn't report directly to you so that should be OK. Give me the background.'

Simon explained Eric's history and how it was peppered with bad judgement calls, drawing parallels between his relationship with Piers, and Eric's relationship with Mike.

'Mike is an interrogator. He doesn't lose his temper and go into intimidator like Piers, but he can be a very hostile critic, even to the point of being a bully. I think the control drama between the two of them needs exposing, because it causes Eric to descend into his lower self and do the most idiotic things. To fight expectations that he'll foul up he tries too hard, gets too anxious, and then a mistake is inevitable. You can help him to pull out of this in much the same way as you're helping me with Piers, I expect.'

'Does Mike have a coach?' asked Angela.

'Yes, he works with Malcolm Manners from your organisation.'

'Good. Maybe somewhere down the line the two executives and the two coaches can get together and negotiate a

114

more helpful reporting relationship. But I'll work with Eric on a one to one basis for a while first,' Angela promised.

'Thanks, Angela. I must go now. Thanks for fitting me in at such short notice.'

They walked out of the park together and down Piccadilly towards their offices. At the Burlington Arcade they paused before parting.

'Just one final point,' said Angela. 'When fearful thoughts about Red Roger creep into your mind, acknowledge them. Then try to get back into your higher self through remembering your power to create your own reality. You pulled Red Roger into your life for a reason, and you can push him out as well. 'Bye for now.'

Simon went straight off to a meeting with Andy and Doug; he spent the rest of the day in his higher self, and enjoyed the energy and peace it gave him. He even managed to have a constructive conversation with Piers, who was initially alarmed at the plans to spend such large sums on resources for the IT department. Simon acknowledged Piers's views, admitted that it was a risk and that the outcome was not certain, but stood his ground. He deflected Piers's jibes and managed to negotiate most of the extra funding he needed. I hope I can keep this up, thought Simon, when he put the phone down.

It was early Friday evening when he finished his telephone conversation with Piers. He was invited to a party at a friend's house in Notting Hill and wondered if he could be bothered to go. It would be a younger crowd, and he wasn't sure if he was in the mood for thirtysomething trendies, but he went home and revived himself in the sauna; then he decided to make a late appearance. He could easily come straight back home if it felt too much like hard work.

When Simon walked into the party he nearly made a quick exit. It was ten in the evening and the party was well under way. The other guests were talking loudly and enthusiastically. They clustered in tight little groups, which Simon did not feel like penetrating. They all looked very young, confident, thrusting and beautiful. He took a glass of champagne from a passing waiter and, leaning against the wall, decided to defy quantum mechanics for once, and be an observer rather than a participant. This amused him for half an hour, and when he finished his champagne he decided to leave.

Just then a nice-smelling creature nudged him from the side. 'Do you want to talk or dance?' it asked.

Simon looked more closely at his new companion, a stunning-looking woman of around his age. 'Let's talk first. I don't like dancing with strangers.'

She introduced herself as Serena Dunn and gave him her life story before dragging him on to the dance floor. Serena was a retired investment banker. She had been a managing director with a small US investment bank called ILD, which had subsequently been bought by one of the bigger banks. After a successful career at the London office she decided she was fed up with corporate politics and the never-ending tensions between London and New York. She had made enough money out of her shares and wise investment of her bonuses in property, and had no need to keep working. Her husband left her three years ago, and at that point she retired from the bank and now worked as a fundraiser three days a week for a charity. 'My work–life balance is great,' she boasted. 'I'm as happy as Larry and as healthy as a person can be.'

'You look pretty good on it,' admitted Simon, looking at her enviously and lustfully. Could this be the sort of well balanced, emotionally healthy woman I would like to have in my life, he wondered.

They danced for a while and then stopped for another drink. Simon was enjoying himself. The disco was thumping out his favourite golden oldies. Serena continued to look good and smell good. 'That must be very expensive perfume you're wearing,' he said. 'You smell good enough to eat.'

'I don't normally allow people to eat me until I've got to know them very well,' said Serena. Simon viewed that remark as a challenge and lightly brushed the tips of her nipples with his hand.

'That's the one thing that could get me to climb down from my principles,' said Serena, stroking his crotch not so lightly.

After a while Simon took her hand and led her upstairs. They looked into one bedroom but there was a cot in there containing a baby. The next bedroom was already occupied by a couple getting to know each other very well. Finally at the top of the house they found a large attic bedroom with a four-poster bed occupied only by a large Persian cat. 'You don't mind sharing, do you?' he asked the cat, and slowly undressed Serena. 'Be gentle with me,' he said as they sank on to the soft quilt. They had a good time; Serena kept up a stream of instructions, but nonetheless proved to be an exciting lover.

Some time later when they were getting dressed Serena said, 'You certainly know how to play a tune on my piano. With a little more practice and tuition you could be a virtuoso. Do call if you want to become the world's most accomplished lover.' She gave him her card and left. He finished dressing and went downstairs, after saying goodbye to the cat. He looked around for Serena, but she had vanished, so he went home to bed and dreamt of her spanking him because he didn't learn quickly enough.

He did of course call her. Lust got in the way of the subtle early warning signals given out by a controlling personality.

Chapter Thirteen

Preparation for the senior management conference filled the next few weeks to overflowing. Instead of presenting on his own Simon decided to orchestrate a team presentation to include Roger, Carolyn, Verity and Andy. Simon was to start with the vision and strategy, and finish with the results and the way forward. The other directors were to report on how each of their functions was contributing to the overall strategy. Simon's team were thrilled to have the exposure, but it meant hours of joint rehearsals. In among the flurry of preparations Andy and Verity had some tense exchanges about the performance of the IT department. Andy was cautiously optimistic about Doug, while Verity continued to tear her hair out over his department, and its effect on her research teams. Simon found himself standing up for Doug.

'It's early days yet, they're still recruiting. Wait until the new operations manager has joined and is bedded in. Then you should see things speed up.'

Verity continued to be noisily pessimistic, so one day Simon found the opportunity to take her aside for a chat. The subject of the conversation was Doug Allen, but Simon was really seizing the chance to coach Verity on her approach to life.

'You do have a tendency to see the cup as half empty instead of half full,' he said her.

'I know. People have been on at me about it all my adult life. Even my coach is trying to help me to change. However in Doug Allen's case I think my negativity is justified.'

Simon decided to stick to discussing Verity's attitude, rather than descend into an argument over Doug. 'It's not that you aren't sometimes right. It's that your first reaction to any situation tends to be "what can go wrong?" I think that makes it much more likely that things *will* go wrong, as your negative expectations reduce the energy levels and therefore the performance of the other person.'

'I've just begun to work on this with my coach. One month ago I'd have thought you were as batty as a loon to be making a remark like that, but now I am getting a glimmer of understanding.'

'I used to evaluate life in terms of what it lacked or what could go wrong. Angela gave me an exercise to do which has me focusing on what I have to be grateful for, several times a day. It's made me more positive.'

'Actually, I have noticed. You're very much nicer to be around these days.'

Simon was so pleased with the compliment that he nearly forgot what he was going to say next. 'Why don't you try to focus on what you're in favour of, like hitting time targets in IT projects? Do this instead of stressing what you're against, like the way IT projects slip against targets. Everything you have to say can be restated in a way that puts you in support of something rather than against its opposite.'

'That won't make the IT problem go away.'

'There you go again,' said Simon, still refusing to get drawn into a petty argument over Doug Allen. 'Your first reaction to a new idea or situation tends to be negative.'

This made Verity sit up and think. 'You know, you do have a point. It is a bad habit. I wouldn't like it if your initial reaction to everything I said were negative. I promise to do what I can to correct it. It might stick in my throat, but I'm going to be positive about what I hope Doug Allen can achieve for us.'

Simon left it at that, knowing that she would try very hard.

Carolyn was rather preoccupied throughout the rehearsals, although her speech was the most professional of all. She was also planning another one, the 'goodbye forever' speech to Piers. She even said Piers instead of Andecis twice while rehearsing her presentation. Everyone, apart from Simon, was mystified by this strange slip.

Simon continued to be enthusiatic and confident, but sometimes became ratty. In doing so he laid himself open to an occasional poke in the ribs from Verity, who had taken his remarks very much to heart and did not want him setting her a bad example. He was not getting enough sleep. Serena had a lot to do with this. Simon called her his 'play it again, Sam' babe. Working only a three-day week left her with a lot of energy for leisure activities, of which sex was the main one.

'Why don't you go back to investment banking and work a full week?' suggested Simon. 'Then we'd be more compatible.'

Serena had no sympathy for his need for sleep. 'I believe lovers should be very close and very physical,' she said in her emphatic way. 'I have a high need for affection.'

He felt slightly smothered and despaired of ever getting her to see his point of view. Serena thought nothing of waking him up in the early hours of the morning for an extra session of lovemaking, or just for a conversation. When she did this Simon could not go back to sleep again, and felt like death when he had to get out of bed at six o'clock. Finally he banned her from staying the night during the working week.

'You keep such a distance between us,' she complained. 'You're very inconsiderate of my needs.' Simon considered this comment to be rather ironic, but said nothing. Serena enjoyed arguing and sparring with him. She was not as spectacularly badly behaved as Grace had been, but she kept on at it relentlessly; he found he no longer felt so indulgent towards this trait as he once had.

'I'm coming with you to New York!' Serena joyfully announced a few days before the conference. Simon was not sure if this was a good idea, but she was adamant. She had heard that many of the other wives and husbands would be there, especially the partners of the US-based directors. 'There's even a party one evening to which directors' partners are invited,' she said triumphantly. Simon gave in.

The conference was in the Essex House hotel, overlooking Central Park, a fabulous location. Piers's apartment was just around the corner. Simon had a rather grand suite on the twenty-sixth floor. It boasted a large opulent drawing room and dining room. In addition there were three bedrooms, three bathrooms and two kitchens. Little use was made of the kitchens, but the bedrooms were all occupied. Katy and Edward took one each, and he and Serena occupied the third. The children, both on holiday, were to spend a few days with Simon in New York, and then go off to the Hamptons to visit Emily's sister. The trip marked the start of

Katy's round-the-world travels in her gap year. She was awaiting her exam results and hoping to get a place at Oxford in a year's time, to study psychology.

They were all very excited to be in New York. The weather was hot, but not oppressively so. Simon, Serena and the children spent the weekend sightseeing and visiting the Frick gallery and the Metropolitan Museum. Carolyn flew in on Sunday; she was to stay around the corner in the Pier, a more understated but equally lovely hotel. Simon went running with her in Central Park on Monday morning at six. The conference was due to start on Tuesday, which was the day the European team was presenting. Carolyn was more focused on her meeting with Piers than on the conference presentation. 'He's being as affectionate towards me as ever,' she said as they ran round the reservoir in the middle of the park. 'After cold-shouldering me for six months he doesn't seem to have a clue that I'm preparing to call it all off.'

'Empathy isn't exactly his middle name,' said Simon, puffing as he tried to keep up with Carolyn. 'When are you going to speak to him?'

'We're having dinner at Nobu on Tuesday night. I'll do the deed then over a plate of sushi and a glass of Chardonnay.'

When Simon returned to his suite Serena was looking out of the picture windows overlooking the park, Katy and Edward presumably still fast asleep. 'What do you mean by leaving my bed to go running with Carolyn!' she demanded. Simon felt momentarily angry, then decided to let her words pass through him while he remained in his peaceful higher self. He was discovering that it was the only way to deal with Serena.

'Carolyn is my friend and jogging companion,' he said, smiling and kissing her. 'But you are my true love. Besides, after a night with you, I have nothing left in me for other women. Why don't you take up jogging? Then you could come with us.' He bit his tongue after this, realising that was the last thing he wanted. He needn't have worried.

'Exercise is bunk. If you're healthy you don't need it and if you're sick you shouldn't do it.'

He ended the pointless conversation by going to have a shower. After that Serena tried to pick fights with him all day. Simon had meetings with Piers and with his team. Serena wanted him to go shopping with her and the children. He just smiled and said, 'Sorry darlings, duty calls.' Serena bought tickets for all of them to go to the theatre on Monday evening, and then afterwards to dinner at the Jean-George, where they ate a large sumptuous meal of rich food. Simon finally got to sleep at one am.

'I knew it would be a mistake to bring Serena with me,' he muttered to himself as he groped for his razor in the luxurious marble bathroom early the next morning. 'At least she's good company for the children. They're having a whale of a time.' Serena, for all her other faults, was remarkably good with young people. When she was not being critical, she was warm, loving and outgoing, and made herself generally popular. Remembering this Simon felt guilty at harbouring negative thoughts about her.

Adrenaline was pumping through his body as he walked into the hotel restaurant. His team's presentation was the second item on the agenda that day, after opening remarks from Piers. He joined Piers and his team at a table by the window, and ordered scrambled eggs and bacon, looking defiantly at Carolyn, who winked at him over her bowl of fruit. She just sets me a good example, but never criticises, he thought.

As they were finishing their coffee Piers said, 'Well, Simon, I've decided to throw my weight in behind you. I hope you people in tea-break land know what you're doing with this vision and strategy of yours. If you do, you're in a position to give leadership to the rest of the company globally. Give them all you've got, and don't fail me afterwards.'

They all stared at Piers in surprise. 'As thoughts for the day go, that's a good one, Piers,' said Andy.

'See you at tea-break time,' said Carolyn, and walked off to the ladies' room. The tension was having an effect on her bladder.

At 10.30 am Simon began his presentation. His passion and conviction carried the day, and he forgot his nerves. Halfway through his opening speech there was a slight disturbance at the back of the room; at first he ignored it, then from the corner of his eye he saw Serena walk in and sit down. She was closely followed by two security guards, who firmly led her out into the hall again. He caught Piers's eye and Piers smiled at him as if to say: 'At it again, Simon?' Simon carried on with his delivery. No doubt a resentful Serena would have to be placated that evening, but for now he would allow nothing to get in the way of a polished delivery.

The rest of his team also performed well, receiving warm applause. The time spent rehearsing and arguing over the content of the presentation had not been wasted.

Simon spent the rest of the day in impromptu meetings with directors from around the world. He and his team had created a lot of interest, and the global heads each found an opportunity to speak to him over the two days of the conference. He had drawn up a list of senior sponsors to target, but in the event they all sought him out. He arranged to return to New York in six weeks' time for fuller discussions with three of them. When he walked into his suite in the early evening he was on a high.

Serena's mood did not match his. The security guards had not allowed her anywhere near the conference room for the rest of the day. 'What sort of a chief executive are you,' she said tersely, 'if your partner cannot sit quietly at the back and hear you speak? I was publicly humiliated and you did nothing about it.'

Simon chose to be patient. 'The guards were instructed to let in no one other than company employees. I'm sorry you had such an unpleasant experience, but they have to be careful. Remember I'm on Red Roger's death list. You could have been an animal rights activist with a gun strapped to your chest for all they knew. Let's have a drink and forget about it.' He poured them each a glass of white wine and settled back on the plush sofa to savour the day. But Serena would not let up.

'I've had such a boring day here on my own. The children left for the Hamptons at ten o'clock and I've had nothing to do since. You could have pulled some strings to let me in to the conference. You're so thoughtless where I'm concerned that it probably didn't occur to you.'

'You're right about one thing,' said Simon, nearing the end of his patience. 'It didn't occur to me. No one else had a partner in there. It's a conference for Andecis directors only. It would be completely against the rules for me to try to get you in. People would think I was mad.'

'I don't give a fig for corporate rules. I've had them up to here, which is why I left ILD and became semi-retired.'

123

'Well, I'm not semi-retired,' snapped Simon, annoyed with himself for losing his cool. 'And I do give a fig.'

Serena glared at him over her glass of wine. Suddenly Simon found the prospect of spending an evening with her distinctly unappealing. Here I am, being challenged and criticised again, he realised. But this time by a self-centred, demanding woman.

Serena, unaware of Simon's thoughts, began to cool down. 'What are we doing tonight?' she asked. 'Is there a conference party or dinner?' Simon had an inspiration. 'The conference party is tomorrow night, if you remember. Tonight I have to leave you on your own, I'm afraid. I'm due to join Andy, Verity and Roger for a debrief over dinner. Please order yourself whatever you like from room service, or have a meal in the restaurant. I'm sorry I can't be with you, but I won't be late.' Simon had no plans to dine with his colleagues, but he knew that he would have a much better time with them than with Serena.

Serena became coldly angry. 'Didn't you forget to include Carolyn? Surely she's the star attraction.'

'No, she's dining with Piers,' said Simon. He went into the bathroom, shut the door and using his mobile phone, arranged to go with the gang to Asia de Cuba. When he left the suite Serena was sitting in a corner of the drawing room sulking. He kissed her goodbye and left, his heart lightening as he shut the room door behind him. 'Why do I feel so controlled when I'm in a relationship?' he asked himself as the lift descended to the lobby.

The four of them had an amusing evening at Asia de Cuba. They sat at the centre table reserved for singles, and chatted up the bright young things who were dining there. They ate an outrageously unhealthy meal of fillet steak, lobster and noodles, and drank nearly a bottle of wine a head. When the time came to go Simon could hardly move. With some guilt, he remembered that he had not wished Carolyn good luck with her evening.

When they got back to the Essex House, she was sitting waiting for him in the lobby. After the other three had gone to bed he took Carolyn into a quiet corner of the lounge and ordered two coffees. 'I won't sleep tonight anyway,' she said, 'so I might as well enjoy a nice cappuccino.' Her make-up was streaked with tears.

124

'It all happened just as I imagined it would. Piers listened politely, asked me a few questions to make sure he understood me clearly, then said that I was a wonderful person. He simply didn't respond to my ultimatum that we should marry or part. He didn't even consider it worthy of an answer. It's all over, Simon. I really know where I stand now. I feel absolutely terrible, panic-stricken at facing the future alone, and broken-hearted. I had no idea it would hit me so hard.'

At that point Serena walked up to them. 'Are you coming to bed now, Simon?' she asked coldly, ignoring Carolyn. 'If not, can I join you?'

'No to both, I'm afraid, Serena,' said Simon, 'but I won't be long.' Serena turned and marched out of the lobby.

'You shouldn't have done that,' said Carolyn, starting to laugh through her tears. 'That's one lady who takes herself very seriously. I feel guilty about causing the row you're going to have in a few minutes.'

'You're more important to me than she is,' said Simon, surprising himself. 'I'll stay here with you till dawn if you need me to.'

'Don't do that, darling. I don't want to have to give key evidence at a murder trial.'

They talked for another half an hour. Eventually Simon went up to his suite and walked into the bedroom where Serena was lying in bed with her eyes wide open. 'No more fuss please, Serena,' he said. 'I've had enough for today.' Once he had removed his clothes he fell into the bed and was snoring within minutes. Serena might have tried to make love to him, but if she did he was blissfully unaware.

He overslept the next morning, and only just made it to the hall as the conference was starting. Mercifully Serena had remained fast asleep while he dressed, so he had been spared an early-morning confrontation. At the mid-morning coffee break he noticed that there were two message for him. One was from Carolyn.

Sorry, I just can't face Piers today. I'm flying back to London this morning. Please make my apologies to everyone.

Piers walked up to him as he was reading it. 'Where is Carolyn?' he asked. Then he spotted the note, recognised Carolyn's handwriting, took it from Simon and read it. 'Sorry

125

to be so rude as to read your mail,' he said, looking concerned, 'it's just that I happen to know that Carolyn is going through a bad time in her personal life. She has a bit of a down on me at present. Much as I try, she won't let me near her to help her. Simon, can I ask you to be her guardian angel and see her through the next few months?'

Simon stared at him in fascination. This man is so cool, he thought. He knows I know, yet he refuses to be open with me about it.

'I'll take good care of her,' he said, and as Piers walked away read the second message. It was from Serena.

I have a tummy bug or possibly food poisoning. I've had a terrible night, and am totally dehydrated. I've finished all of the mineral water in the minibar. Please bring me some more.

So that's what I missed by sleeping so soundly, thought Simon, with relief. Surely she could call room service herself and ask for some more water? Then he softened and realised that she probably was feeling starved of attention. 'Can I see you in half an hour?' he said to the global head of research, who was hoping to speak to him. Feeling rather pressurised, he left the conference and went up to see Serena. He took three bottles of mineral water with him and asked the concierge to arrange for someone to send some rehydration salts to the suite.

Serena looked a bit tired, but not very ill. 'I think the worst is over,' she said. 'But I'll have to stay here in the suite, just in case I get caught short. So I'll have to spend another boring, lonely day on my own.'

'That's probably a good idea,' he said, ignoring the attempt to make him feel guilty. 'You need to rest up for the party tonight. It would be a shame to miss that.'

'I'll come if I possibly can, but I make no promises. I had such an awful night; I'm quite weak now. I don't know how you managed to sleep through it all.'

'Alcohol-induced oblivion,' said Simon, preparing to go. 'Have a good sleep this afternoon and you'll be your dynamic self again tonight.'

'We'll see. Thank you for coming up to see me. I appreciate you tearing yourself away from the conference for me.

126

Although I would have appreciated some TLC last night even more.'

'Call room service if you need anything else,' said Simon as he left. He went back into the conference but found it hard to concentrate, thinking instead of his relationship with Serena. She has been demanding and controlling from the start, he admitted. We began to argue over whose needs would be met right from the second time we made love. In the first week of what should have been our tender new relationship we started to bicker. She keeps criticising me and trying to get me to shape up. I keep trying to create more distance, to protect myself from being smothered. She then feels pushed away and becomes even more demanding and critical.

What's going on? Even my marriage to Emily didn't start out like this. We had some really happy times for the first few years, and there was always mutual respect and fairness. I either get pulled down to Serena's level and bicker with her, or I expend huge amounts of effort trying to keep my cool. I'll see if I can get to the bottom of it with Angela. She is bound to have some insight that will make everything abundantly clear.

Serena managed to recover in time for the party, as Simon knew she would. She looked a bit pale, but aggressively eye-catching in a pink sequinned Versace evening dress. Although she was slightly reserved at first, her natural gregariousness soon came through and she began to have a good time.

Piers was a marvellous host. With his elegant wife at his side, he worked the room, charming everyone. He was on very good form, full of fun and warmth. Carolyn ended the relationship, thought Simon, watching him. Yet she is broken-hearted while he is untouched by it all. He must have an electric pump instead of a heart.

At one point Piers came over on his own, and had a word with Simon. 'You really pick them, don't you?' he said, looking at Serena doing the limbo on the dance floor and screaming with laughter as she fell flat on her back. 'That one will never make you a good corporate wife.'

'I know. Don't worry, she won't last.'

'I don't know how you manage it. But you seem to have a knack for picking the most amazingly self-obsessed women as your girlfriends.'

'Very perceptive of you,' said Simon, taking another glass

of champagne from a passing tray, carried by a smiling young waitress. 'Actually you've got it the wrong way round, they pick me.'

'Good looks aren't enough you know, they need to have some maturity and depth as well.'

'You mean, like all the babes you keep boasting to me about?' Simon could not resist making this jibe. He didn't care if he got sacked on the spot; he couldn't let Piers get away with that remark.

Piers looked at Simon for a while, then chuckled. 'You don't really believe that crap, do you, Simon? I invent those women as a way of competing with you, the Romeo of the pharmaceutical world.'

Simon was completely silenced, unsure whether to believe Piers or not. He remembered him saying once: 'When you're accused of adultery, there are three things you must do; deny, deny and deny.' Maybe he was trying to trick Simon into telling Carolyn that her lover had not been unfaithful after all. Maybe he was telling the truth.

Piers smiled. He was obviously in a very expansive mood. 'I see you can't decide whether to believe me or not. I know you're worrying about Carolyn. And I know you know about us, because she told me. I might kill you one day because she's so fond of you and I'm jealous, but for now I need you alive to look after her. The issue for Carolyn is not my unfaithfulness, it's my inability to commit to her and to spend the rest of my life with her. She doesn't appreciate that the love and friendship I have to offer is worth far more than the selfish and demanding love of a husband.'

Having had far too much selfish and demanding love from Serena, Simon conceded to himself that Piers had a point. 'Time will sort that one out,' he said. 'It's really none of my business and I won't interfere.'

Things have moved on for me this week, he thought as he dragged Serena off to bed in the early hours of the morning.

'You are *so* inconsiderate to make me leave such a good party,' she grumbled.

'Stop moaning and behave like the invalid you say you are,' he ordered.

It turned out that she wasn't too ill to make love for almost an hour before he fell into an exhausted sleep.

Chapter Fourteen

Simon sat very still in the meeting room at the Compleat Angler. He was there, with the rest of the UK board of Andecis, taking part in the leadership development programme. Each one of his colleagues had taken centre stage for around fifteen minutes, listing their strengths and weaknesses, and receiving feedback from the others. It was a tough exercise, supportive but hard-hitting. There was a lot of trust in the room, created partly by Simon's openness. However no one was holding back on the truth, however discomforting.

Verity had been told that she was a master organiser, but inclined to be pessimistic, and complaining. Roger learnt that he was forward-looking and professional, but far too inclined to live in Simon's pocket. Peter, the financial director, was very thorough and reliable, but nitpicking and timid. Andy was patient, supportive, good at managing complexity, but slow to grasp the nettle when problems occurred. This latter point was a clear reference to Doug Allen. Carolyn was told that she was inspirational, energetic, a brilliant communicator, but inclined to be moody occasionally. Mike learnt that he was seen as a tireless and effective leader of the sales function, but sometimes a bit of a bully.

Now it was Simon's turn. His palms were a bit sweaty, and he felt as if he was about to take off all of his clothes in front of his team. He forgave himself for feeling scared and plunged into the exercise.

'My main strength is the ability to create and share exciting visions of the future, and to make them come true. My emerging strengths are my growing abilities to realise these dreams with a style of leadership that inspires and empowers. My weaknesses lie in what I used to consider my strengths. These are my inclinations to focus single-mindedly on my goals and to fight my way there in a controlling, combative and interfering way. I preferred to have everyone around me performing brilliantly, in exactly the way I expected them to, in pursuit of *my* goals. I now try to lead by giving support, backing, understanding, clarity of direction and an occasional touch on the tiller. I shall listen with great interest to see if you think that I'm really changing in the way that I hope I am, or if I'm simply fooling myself. I will treasure your honest feedback.'

Verity spoke up first. 'Simon, I now find you absolutely inspirational. If anyone can teach me to see the cup as half full instead of half empty, you can.'

'You aren't fooling yourself,' said Carolyn. 'You really are changing. Occasionally we see the old you, as you bark out an order or make a decision without consultation. You did this for example over the decision to do a joint presentation at the New York conference. But because you've created such a climate of empowerment we all feel that we can challenge you, even when you revert to command and control. As it happened, we all wanted to do that presentation with you, so you got no challenges over that. I feel that sometimes you're carried away by your own insights and enthusiasm and then forget that someone else might have a point of view.'

'I agree,' said Andy. 'It's just the way people grow, never in a straight line but in jerky movements, with some backsliding. We're all behind you, Simon; you're creating a lot of loyalty with your vision and your empowering style. Let me just give you a slight touch to your tiller, to use one of your phrases. I know you want to spread responsibility and trust down to appropriate levels in the company, but you've recently done something that works against that. By insisting that board directors have to sign all travel requests, even for flights to Paris, you sent out a message that says only top management have that responsibility and trust. I know we're in a cost-efficiency programme, but we should be getting line managers to do that sort of monitoring, leaving our time freer to be directors rather than managers.'

'I've been working very closely with Simon this summer,' said Roger. 'I endorse everything the rest of you have said. I want to add that I think we have in him a leader who tries, and largely succeeds, in putting very positive beliefs into practice.'

The feedback continued along these lines. Simon felt hugely validated, despite the criticisms, all of which he felt he could do something about anyway.

Later that day Angela turned up. She was a guest speaker on the programme, and spoke to them about what she called the 'authentic power' of a transformational leader.

'Traditional leaders, of the command and control brigade, base their leadership style on the belief that we live in a world of scarcity and unpredictability. This is why each person struggles so deeply with power: the lack of it, the acquisition of it, how one should have it. We need to have power to control a hostile universe. The traditional leader sees power as external. He or she seeks to manipulate their world, and the people in it, to get as much power as they need, to deal with their fear of this hostile universe. The less empowered they feel, deep inside, the more they have the need to control things that are external to them. The irony is that when you seek to dominate another person, you dominate no one, but disempower yourself.

'Contrast that with authentic power, which is based on the belief that the universe is one of plenty, and that we all have the ability to create our own reality. Authentic power feels good. It's doing what you are here on earth to be doing, fulfilling your purpose. It's the freedom to act, not to wield power over others. You look forward to each day. When you experience authentic power you forget to be frightened, whereas when you rely on external power you're always frightened. External power comes and goes. Pursuing it is a full-time job. Authentic power doesn't depend on what happens outside of you, but on what happens inside.

'An authentically empowered person is humble and harmless, with the harmlessness of one who treasures and reveres life, in all its forms. To be harmless is to be so strong, bolstered by the power of your inner beliefs, that there is no fear in you to drive you to defend yourself by attacking others. These are the leaders who inspire, empower and energise those around them to achieve great things and transform their organisations.'

A lively discussion followed. The only director who had

nothing to say was Mike, who sat looking very pensive. Some people were enthusiastic about growing towards a life that was not dominated by fear. Others found it hard to see how they could let go of external power, in a world full of in-competence and danger.

Angela explained. 'When you change your focus away from "how can I protect myself", to "how can I contribute to those around me and to my mission", then you gain authentic power. The moral authority that this attitude gives us creates a starlike quality. It's our humility, our desire to be of service, that makes us stars, not our arrogance. Once you start along this path you'll very quickly experience the peace and power it gives you. Of course you will backslide, and revert to trad-itional ways of thinking and leading. When this happens remember to surrender, to give up your striving and go with the flow of the universe, accepting that you are creating the reality around you anyway. Then you will regain your balance and go back to experiencing real power. Get help and support from each other, from your coaches, from whoever is in your life who can give that help. Transformation is not a solitary journey.'

Mike cornered Simon after this session, and they had a discussion sitting on the patio watching the water from the Thames pour over the weir. 'I have a sense of déjà vu,' said Simon, remembering their last time together in May, on a similarly lovely long summer evening.

'That's because Eric is again the subject of our conver-sation. Except that this time, I realise that I need to add myself to the formula.'

'You had some tough feedback today. How are you holding up, old man?' The reference to Mike's age was a joke. As the youngest member of the European board, he was constantly being teased.

'I must admit I'm not feeling too good right now. But I accept the feedback. My coach has been trying to get me to see how I contribute to Eric's episodes of poor leadership. Angela's remarks about authentic leadership really put the whole thing in context. I felt those points were directed straight at me. The cap fits and I guess I have to wear it.'

Simon's heart went out to Mike, who was being very brave though Simon knew he was smarting like mad inside. Anyone insecure enough deep down inside to need to be a bullying interrogator has to find public criticism devastating. Yet Mike was not trying to defend himself or deny it, he was trying to learn.

'Of all the team you have learnt the most from this workshop,' Simon said to him. 'I expect great things of you and have complete confidence in your ability to overcome these weaknesses. Just remember you're otherwise a very able leader. That should put the criticisms in perspective.'

'Thanks Simon, I needed that.' They then went inside, just as it was starting to drizzle, and joined the others for dinner.

While Simon and his team were dining that night at the Compleat Angler, a meeting of a very different sort was taking place in a garage in the suburbs of Birmingham. Red Roger and his band of three supporters were planning their campaign for the autumn.

'We need to do something dramatic to get the subject of animal rights back into the newspapers and into public debate,' said Fred, puffing at his cigarette.

'What do you think we've been trying to do all year?' asked Kevin.

'A few failed attempts to kill leading scientists and drug company bosses hardly did the trick. They just see us as a load of wankers who couldn't organise an orgy in a whorehouse,' Fred snapped back.

'You mean a piss-up in a brewery, you illiterate old fart,' countered Kevin.

'I'll use my own metaphors if you don't mind.'

Red Roger called the meeting to order. 'Comrades, please. Save your literary debates for a time when we don't have something so fucking serious to discuss.'

'Tom had a go a while back at putting a bomb under Simon Bruce's doormat, but he came home unexpectedly early and Tom had to scuttle off. He went back later but the bloody policeman was there,' Fred complained.

Tom entered the discussion. 'The police are always snooping around the houses of these targets of ours. We'll have to do something a bit out of the ordinary to score a hit. It's time somebody died, someone whose death will make a big splash in the news media.'

'For every animal they tortured they should have one piece

of their body cut off until there's nothing left,' said Red
Roger.

'We're fighting a campaign to end animal experiments, but
you seem to need revenge as well,' Kevin exclaimed.

'I can see his point,' Tom said. 'If a few big names meet a
terrible death it'll put the fear of God into the rest. The drug
companies won't be able to persuade anyone to risk doing
animal experiments afterwards. We'll have won!'

Red Roger dug a piece of wax out of his ear and snarled
at his mates. 'I'm not just in this to stop animal testing, I
want it to be payback time for these bastards. I want them
to feel the terror and pain that they've inflicted on their
victims over the years. I'll really enjoy making one of them
squeal for his life.'

'You're a bloody nutter,' growled Kevin.

'Well, whatever our motives we need to sharpen up our act
and start scoring a few successes,' Fred pointed out.

'Let me give it some thought. An idea is beginning to form.'
Red Roger, refusing to say any more about what this might
mean, brought the meeting to an end. He headed off on a
date with his longstanding girlfriend in the Bull and Parrot.

Carolyn and Simon had a chat in his office after the leadership programme. 'I thought it was a great success,' Carolyn
said, sitting on the edge of Simon's large desk.

'Thank you. How are you these days, Carolyn? I haven't
seen much of you lately and I've missed our runs together. I
go on my own but it's not the same.'

'I've been travelling around Europe, so I haven't been here
that much for the last month. I'm slowly getting over the
heartbreak. I still think of Piers, but not so much as I used to.
My old energy is coming back, now that it's not draining away
into my yearning for him. He avoids me, which is helping me
to recover. The less I see of him, the less I brood about him.
There are no more personal e-mails and phone calls, only the
occasional business discussion. Either he's terrified that I'll
do a Grace Lee on him, or he's being a good friend and
staying out of my life to help me to get over him. I prefer to
think it's the latter.'

'As usual you're an inspiration to me, Carolyn,' Simon said,
amazed that she could be so devoid of bitterness over Piers.
'Shall we have a run together tonight after work?'

'Fine. I'll come and get you at 6 pm. That will give you an incentive to manage your time today like a superstar!'

It was Friday, and Serena was due to turn up at Simon's house at seven to cook them some dinner, and get their weekend together started. They'd had a conversation on the return flight from New York. He'd told her that he did not like her constant criticisms and complaints, and that they would have to stop if she wanted to continue seeing him. He was pretty blunt, thinking that it would cause an explosion, but hoping it would clear the air. To his surprise Serena took his words calmly.

'I know I shouldn't do it, but it's a lifelong habit and I'm too old to change. Just tell me when I'm annoying you. Part of the reason why I didn't get any further in the bank was that I was very unpolitical and told people what I thought of them whenever I felt the urge.'

Her response disarmed Simon, so he let the subject drop.

Serena did improve for a while. Then she got worse, in the sense that she started criticising him and picking on him in public. Simon got back into that familiar mode where he either descended to her level and snapped back at her, or expended a lot of energy dealing with her in a civilised way when he was churning with irritation inside. He spoke to her about it again, and she shrugged her shoulders and said, 'You can't teach an old dog new tricks,' and took him off to bed where she tried very hard to please him. She was finding it harder and harder to do that these days. Ground down by her negativity, Simon's infatuation was disappearing.

He picked up the phone and dialled her number. 'Serena, I'm afraid I won't be home tonight until much later than I thought,' he said. 'I'm going for a run with Carolyn, and by the time I've had a shower and a drink it'll probably be after nine. Is that a problem for you?'

'So she's back in your life again, is she?'

Simon groaned inwardly and said, 'Yes, she is, as my running companion. The only reason we haven't been running together lately is that she's been away. I'll see you after nine.' He put the phone down, knowing that everything they didn't fight about now would be on the agenda that evening.

Simon bent Carolyn's ear on the subject while they were having a cold lager in the pub after their run. 'I should have

discussed it with Angela but there have been so many important business matters to work through that I haven't had the
time to bring it up. I feel slightly guilty that I haven't been
able to make a go of this relationship, and that I'm going to
have to hurt Serena. She's a good person in many ways,
always on the lookout to help others, and very friendly to
everyone, regardless of who they are. She does wonders for
the charity she works for.'

'I can understand you feeling guilty because it's not nice to
have to hurt anyone. But she's pulled you into her life for a
reason, so maybe she has to learn a lesson from the rejection
you're about to give her.'

'I've tried to warn her that I find her criticisms hard to take,
but that's one lesson she isn't prepared to learn.'

'You've done your best. There's no need to feel guilty.
Maybe the shock of the parting will give her the incentive to
change. If I were you I wouldn't have lasted two weeks on the
receiving end of her interrogations and jibes.'

'Interrogations! That's it, it's my old control drama again.
She's the interrogator and I'm busily playing aloof as much as
I can. That's why her negative behaviour has such a dampen-
ing effect on my energy. She pulls energy out of me with her
questions and hostility, and it takes a disproportionate
amount of effort to respond to her when she's doing that.'

'I can just imagine.'

'I don't want to continue my relationship with Serena, but
at least I can be compassionate and kind in the way I say
goodbye. Carolyn, you have scored as a super coach again.
Let's have another lager to celebrate. And will you come over
and spend Sunday afternoon with me, and wander round a
museum or play tennis, whatever you fancy? I'll be on my
own by then, without a partner, and might be in need of
company.'

'It's a date, but I won't have another lager. I think you
should go home and do the deed. There's no point in torturing her by keeping her waiting too long. But one last thing
before you go, Simon. Try to forgive yourself, both for the
times you snapped at her and for the fact that you're
dumping her. You've done your best. All you can do now is
to learn from your experiences. You don't need to beat yourself black and blue.'

So Simon went home and did the deed. He was as kind as

he could be and blamed his own inadequacy for the pre-mature ending of the affair. He just explained it away as a recurring pattern in his life that he was bad at sustaining relationships. Serena, true to herself to the last, agreed that he was inadequate and took no blame for anything. She repacked her bags and left after dinner. She looked sad as she walked to the front door, and Simon was feeling extremely guilty, until she fired her parting shot. 'By the way, Simon, you know those moles you have all over the front of your body? You should get them looked at in case you have skin cancer.'

I've done the right thing, he thought. I couldn't live with that for a moment longer. Then he thought how sad it was that she had such a strong need to keep putting people down that she destroyed relationships, and compassion replaced the anger.

He got ready for bed; just before turning off the light he saw that the message light was flashing. There was only one message. Since he had taken up with Serena his friends had not been issuing the usual number of invitations. They had obviously found her a bit feisty, especially when she started the campaign of putting him down in public. Perhaps he should have another party to get things going again. He listened to the message, hoping it was an invitation, or a call from Katy who was now in South America, and not due to come home until Christmas. It was none of these. The Birmingham accent sounded over the phone. 'You're at the top of my death list now, Simon Bruce. Take action before it's too late.'

Chapter Fifteen

Two weeks later an alarmed Angela confronted Simon in her office, and he found himself rather taken aback by a side of her he had not seen before.

'What do you mean, you haven't told Inspector Larkman!' she cried. 'Do you want them to kill you?'

'Hang on a minute, Angela,' Simon tried to defend himself. 'First of all I've been on his death list for over six months, an honour I share with many others in my field, and no one has yet been killed. I've had these extremists threatening me for most of my working life, and nothing has ever happened. Secondly, I'm already enjoying police protection. There are plain-clothes officers at my house and sometimes at the office or the sites I visit. I've been taught how to be careful about checking for car bombs and letter bombs. Thirdly, I expect to be safe. If I have positive visions about my personal safety then of course I'll create a safe reality. So I've decided not to give Red Roger the satisfaction of causing any extra worry.'

'This reminds me of the conversation I had with my son over visioning success in his exams while lying watching television instead of revising. All of the work we've done towards creating a desired reality for you has involved both imagination and practical work. The way I see this is that God keeps trying to get you to take more action to keep yourself safe, and you keep ignoring Him!'

'OK, I see your point. I guess I was becoming a bit complacent. I'll phone Inspector Larkman as soon as I get back to the office.'

'Cross your heart and hope to die?'

'You have my word.'

They sat looking at each other for a few moments. Angela had a way of allowing the occasional silence for Simon to reflect on something important that had just gone on between them. This was one of those moments. Finally he remembered the good news that he had come to tell her before the exchange over Red Roger had pushed it to the back of his mind.

'Now for a more happy subject. The news from Verity is that the results from the recent trials for Time Warp are excellent. They are genuinely hopeful that the drug will get a smooth passage to acceptance from the regulators later this week. We're all geared up to manufacture and market, so it's crossed fingers until then. We really cannot afford another disaster this year; this will be a real triumph for us if we're successful. Apparently Doug's department pulled out all the stops and gave them the IT support they needed in good time. The new operations manager for the IT department hit the decks running. The headhunters found us a perfect fit for that brief. He's getting results in the department even before they've recruited all the staff they say they need. I'm now full of hope for next year.'

'That's really good news. I bet Piers is pleased.'

'He's overjoyed. He's giving me credit for pulling things round, and I'm having to keep reminding him and the others who deserves the real credit. I think that it's Andy and the IT team.'

Angela looked fondly at Simon. 'Take some for yourself too. You were very courageous and took a risk with keeping Doug and pouring all that money into extra people for his team.'

Simon smiled. 'I'll take a gold star. We have a long way to go yet, but I think we're well positioned to go forward. It's very gratifying to have Piers patting me on the back instead of bellowing at me. He still sometimes has a go at me, but I've got him to stop doing it in public.'

'How have you done that?' Angela enquired.

'I simply asked him to stop. I told him it had a bad effect on my self-esteem, and undermined my leadership position in Europe. He agreed that was the last thing either of us wanted, especially at such a critical time for the company. But he did admit that he might have some lapses because it was an old habit. It put me in mind somewhat of Serena's reaction when I spoke to her about her constant criticisms.'

'Are you still seeing her?'

'No. She called recently and asked if we could get together and talk things over. She didn't think that things were completely hopeless between us. I told her I would consider her suggestion and I did. I was tempted out of compassion for her to have an amicable discussion and see if we couldn't be just friends. Then I thought, no, it wouldn't work. I really want to get to a stage in my life where I leave these control dramas behind me, and stop having relationships with interrogators. Unlike Piers, she's too caught up in her drama to change, and I want to use my energy for positive purposes, not for sparring with her. So I called back and said a final goodbye.'

'How do you feel towards her?'

'Compassionate mostly.'

'Good, I'm glad that you're able to feel that, and not the anger or fear that drives you into your aloof drama with people like her. That's a step forward for you. I hope it means that you won't need to pull another person like that into your life. When someone acts in a way that you find disagreeable, your hurt, anger or fear is how you choose to process that person's behaviour. You do have another choice, and that seems to be the one you have taken in this case. Instead of judging the difficult person, you can accept them for precisely where they are on their own growth path. This will eliminate your need to be upset by them, and you can forgive them. It's these everyday decisions that keep you up there where you want to be in your higher self. You're doing a lot these days to keep yourself in a peaceful place.'

'Things are going the way I want them to right now. Maybe I've cracked it.'

'The universe has a way of dealing with people who think that they've cracked it. It brings another growth opportunity into your life.'

'I know that's meant to be a warning, and I take it as such and will remember to be more humble. However I do feel ready for any new growth experiences the universe has in store for me, especially if they involve pretty women.'

They both laughed and parted on a high note. Angela called in to see her colleague Chris in his office before writing up the coaching session.

140

'I'm worried about Simon's safety,' she said. 'You know he's receiving death threats from animal rights activists.'

'Yes, it's been in the papers.'

'It's really shaken him up, as it would do you or me. But he seems to swing between panic and complacency. Neither state produces the sort of mental alertness he needs to keep himself safe.'

Chris stroked his chin for a bit. 'I suppose it's all a bit too much for him, and he's swinging back and forth before he settles down into some sort of equilibrium.'

'I guess he'll settle down eventually. It's an awful thing to have hanging over you, and it's really testing his ability to maintain his newfound peace of mind.'

Back in her office Angela included a reflective comment in her notes on Simon. 'I've just realised, it's I who needs to have faith that Simon will be safe, and that whatever happens to him will be something that he can handle and learn from.' She then got herself a hot chocolate from the machine, and let the soothing drink give her some comfort.

Simon rushed back to his Mayfair office, realising that he was late for his run with Carolyn. When he got to his office a pleasant sight greeted him. Carolyn's lovely bare legs were in full view. She had already changed into her running shorts, and was sitting in his chair with her feet up on his desk, reading the *Evening Standard*. 'Hello, darling,' she said, 'are you fit?'

Simon quickly changed in the gents; they drove into Hyde Park and parked the car. It was already getting dark. They had tickets for the theatre later and wanted to make a quick getaway after their run so that they could shower and get to the Aldwych in time. As they set off they didn't notice another car, a battered old Ford Fiesta, pull up beside the Mercedes. A thin wiry man with long straggly reddish-brown hair got out, carrying a Tesco shopping bag and muttering to himself. Had they been within earshot they would have heard that he muttered in a Birmingham accent.

It was mid-October and autumn was just setting in. The leaves on the oaks and beeches were beginning to turn, and were glowing with colour. They ran round the Serpentine and then up into Kensington Gardens. The flowerbeds were looking a bit tired but the grass was very green and provided a refreshing background to the autumn leaves. It wasn't raining for a change, and they could still see the colours dimly in the twilight at the start of the run. Forty minutes later when they got back to the car it was completely dark. Simon then realised that he had forgotten to call Inspector Larkman.

He felt that old sense of foreboding welling up and, although he tried to think cheerful thoughts, it would not go away. He opened up the boot of the car and they both pulled out their tracksuits and put them on. It was cold now that the sun had set. They got into the car and Simon put the keys into the ignition.

'Don't make a sound. Put your hands on your head, and obey me in everything I tell you to do, otherwise you're dead meat.' A Birmingham voice spoke these words menacingly from the back seat. Simon and Carolyn, frightened out of their minds, did everything they were told.

'I'm going to cover your eyes and mouths with tape, and then I'm going to drug you, one at a time. If either of you struggles or makes a false move, the other dies. I'm only drugging you for the length of the journey so that you don't know where I'm taking you. I'll deal with you first, Simon.' Carolyn watched in horror as the tape went over Simon's mouth and eyes, and then a dirty rag, which smelt strongly, was put over his nose. In seconds he slumped in his seat. She then had to allow herself to be subjected to the same treatment. Soon they were both dead to the world.

When they woke up they felt terrible, nauseous and very uncomfortable. Red Roger had tied their hands together behind their backs. He had also tied their feet together very tightly, so that the rope was cutting into the flesh. He had left the tapes over their eyes and mouths. When he saw them stir he removed the tapes and spoke to them. 'Now you know what it feels like to be a poor little animal trussed up and ready for experiments.'

Simon was about to tell him about the humane methods they used in their laboratories, but Carolyn, who was sitting on the floor very close to him, found a way of nudging him, and he kept quiet. Red Roger had nothing more to say. He went to sleep and snored the loudest, most revolting snore either of them had ever heard. Needless to say neither slept at all that night. Red Roger slept fitfully, and awoke several times, but just as Carolyn and Simon were about to doze off, the snoring started again.

The room got light slowly the next morning. It never got very light, because the only window had shutters, which were closed. There were three doors, one opposite the window, and one at either end of the room. One led to a very smelly lavatory, and the other, they discovered later, to a kitchen. The door opposite the window was locked, and there was no key. Red Roger never used it so they never found out what lay behind it.

'I'm bursting for the loo,' said Carolyn. Only dehydration had kept her from needing to go earlier.

Red Roger walked over to where Carolyn was lying. He knelt down beside her, took a penknife out of his pocket, opened it up and stuck it into her nostril. Simon watched in helpless horror as a small drop of blood trickled down over her mouth. Carolyn kept still, waiting for her nostril to be sliced open. But Red Roger just snarled at her and said, 'You mean you want to use the toilet. Call spade a spade.'

'Yes please, Roger.' Carolyn was shaking but very keen to be compliant and keep the peace. She was not immediately successful. Red Roger's menacing snarl reappeared, and the penknife was waved in the air, though not reinserted in her nostril.

'My name is Red, Roger is my surname. I won't have you calling me by my surname as if you are some poncy public-school teacher.'

'Many apologies, Red. May I please use the toilet?' Finally Red Roger gave in and untied them so that they could both relieve themselves. He tied their feet again when they were finished, but left their hands free so that they could eat the breakfast he brought them from the kitchen. Breakfast was two slices of plastic white bread covered with margarine. They ate hungrily. 'I never thought sliced white bread could taste so good,' Simon muttered while Red Roger was in the kitchen making them all very strong tea.

Simon noticed that Carolyn's hand was shaking as she fed herself. He stroked her arm when Red Roger was looking the other way. He felt utterly helpless. Carolyn had the temerity to ask meekly for water, and Red grudgingly brought them some in the teacups. The water tasted of tea but no one complained. They both peered through the kitchen door whenever Red went through to get food, and could see that it had windows, and also a back door leading out into a small rear yard. They seemed to be in a small, badly kept cottage, and their quick glances through the kitchen window told them that they were in the countryside. When Red came back into the room they both pretended that they had not been looking in that direction. They didn't want him to notice how keenly they were already thinking of how to escape.

The day dragged on and on. 'No one ever told me how boring it is to be kidnapped,' murmured Simon at one point when Red was in the loo.

'We must be very obedient and compliant and let him feel that he's totally in charge. That way he may begin to relax his guard somewhat,' Carolyn said. Simon went along with this.

Unfortunately Red seemed to enjoy inflicting pain and fear. Every now and again he came over to one of them and gave them a small cut in the arm, or face, which was just deep enough to draw blood. As he saw the blood he roared with laughter. It was terrifying. The snarl on his face and the glazed stare of his eyes added to the menace. Each time he approached with the penknife they did not know whether he would just nick the skin, or cut them badly. Some of the cuts went deep, and they hurt. The mixture of terror and suspense, with long spells of boredom, made for a pretty awful sort of a day. Later on hunger was added to their discomfort. In the early evening Simon plucked up his courage and asked Red if they could have some more food.

'Food, you fucking fat cat, why should I bother to feed you when you're probably going to die anyway!' Carolyn let out a little gasp of horror, and Simon could tell from Red's expression that he was pleased with the impact of his words. I hope he said that for effect rather than because he meant it, thought Simon, hardly able to bear the suspense.

Later that evening Red brought them some Spam sandwiches. That's how it was for every meal. Red fed them erratically, but he was consistent with the sandwiches. They all had hearty fillings of margarine and Spam. Red did not eat Spam, being a vegetarian of course. His own sandwiches seemed to contain hummus. At least that's what Simon judged the grey stuff to be that oozed out between the slices as he ate and splattered his already dirty jumper.

'I think he's trying to make a point,' muttered Simon as he ate his slimy, disgusting Spam sandwich. Red's cups of tea were strong, hot and sweet, although as infrequent as the food. No one complained. Carolyn occasionally asked for water, which she sometimes got, but mostly didn't.

Red had lots of intense conversations on his mobile phone in the kitchen. He was discussing strategy with Kevin. They were arguing over whether Red should torture and kill his victims, or do as Kevin suggested, and demand animal rights concessions in return for their release. On one occasion Simon heard a muffled shout of, 'No, you're too soft, they need to die slowly.' Simon's hair stood on end and he felt slightly faint and nauseous. When he looked over at Carolyn he saw the terror in her eyes; he pulled her to him and kissed her on the top of her head. Neither spoke.

Red had violent mood swings, and abused them verbally about their treatment of animals when his mood was bad. Simon was not sure what he was trying to achieve by the kidnapping, but Carolyn thought she knew what was going on. 'Look at his eyes,' she whispered while he was in the kitchen. 'He's either mad, or on drugs. He has no humanity in those eyes at all. You just can't relate to him as a human being. I think he is very dangerous and that he doesn't have a clear purpose, but is making it up as he goes along.'

'He planned the kidnapping though,' said Simon.

'Yes, but having got us here I'm not sure if he's worked out what to do next.'

As if on cue Red came back in from the kitchen, locked the door behind him with a Chubb key, which he sometimes forgot to do, and started to yell at them, waving his penknife. When he'd finished Carolyn said, 'You're right about everything, Red. We are completely in your power and it's your decision as to what to do with us.'

Simon was horrified, and thought Red would take this as an invitation to kill them. But to his surprise it had a calming effect. Later, when Red was out of the room, Carolyn explained her strategy.

'I once read an article about dealing with psychopaths. It said you must always make them feel that they have complete power over you. That's your only hope of avoiding the sort of fear that makes them decide to kill you. If you can help them to feel less fear, and higher self-esteem, then they may not need to do their worst.'

After that Simon joined Carolyn in her effort to make Red

Roger feel in control. Eventually, he began to relax with them a little. First he did not bother to tie Carolyn back again after a visit to the loo. Later he did the same with Simon. They both sat unmoving on the floor, not daring to believe their luck but not wanting to do anything to antagonise Red. He acknowledged their new freedom at the next meal of Spam sandwiches.

'You'll have noticed that you're no longer tied. Just don't try anything funny. I have guards outside this place, so even if you did escape you wouldn't get far. You won't get out through the window; it has a lock and even I don't know where the key is. The two doors leading out of this room are both kept locked. Let me warn you that if you try anything stupid the consequences will be very bad for you. As long as you keep behaving yourselves, I'll leave you free in the daytime, and only tie you up at night.'

'Don't worry, Red,' Simon assured him. 'We wouldn't be so stupid as to try to thwart you in any way.'

For a while the atmosphere was slightly less tense after that exchange. Simon kept saying to himself, I can see peace instead of this, and tried to stay in his higher self and leave his fear behind. When he was in his higher self he was able to look upon the kidnapping as an experience he had pulled into his life so that he could learn a lesson. Just what that lesson was escaped him for the time being, but he had a feeling that he would be able to see it in the fullness of time. Didn't Nietzsche say that whatever doesn't kill outright strengthens, as long as you take the right attitude towards it? His thoughts rambled on. Unfortunately the discomfort and boredom all too often brought him back down into his lower self where he felt fear, anger and frustration. Carolyn was a great support to him, sometimes lightening the atmosphere with attempts to be humorous. She couldn't keep it up all the time, though, because at intervals she too succumbed to gloom and despair.

'Thank goodness there are no mirrors in here,' she muttered once over Red Roger's afternoon-nap snores. 'I must look an absolute mess.'

Simon looked at her in the dim light. There were dark rings under her eyes, and her face and hair were becoming extremely greasy. There was also dried blood in places where it had oozed from the cuts. He had seen her looking better.

'Your fine bone structure continues to make you look

beautiful,' he said chivalrously. 'I can't imagine anyone I would rather be kidnapped with.' He realised he really meant that.

'It's not fair,' Carolyn went on. 'You're just looking increasingly rugged with your growing beard and messy hair. Oh, how I wish we could find a way of getting in touch with the police!'

'I don't know if it would help much, because we haven't the faintest idea where we are.'

Carolyn's face darkened in acknowledgement of that truth, and Simon wished he hadn't said it.

After a few seconds Carolyn pulled herself together and Simon could tell by the changed expression on her face that she was feeling a bit better. 'Have you ever discussed higher self, lower self with Angela?' she asked.

'Yes, as a matter of fact I've just been thinking about it. It does help me sometimes not to panic or be too depressed, but it's bloody difficult to stay up there when you're tired and uncomfortable.'

'I know, I slide down into the depths all too easily.'

'Maybe we can help each other to stay up there. Let's remember what we have to be grateful for.'

'Good thinking, Moriarty. I'm mostly grateful for having you with me, and second on the list is the fact that I've still got my nose.'

'I'm pretty glad to still be alive, and to be fed occasionally.'

'Now that I'm in my higher self it's possible to be more optimistic that something will give and we'll get out of this place alive.'

'Me too. I'm going to keep visioning Red Roger being handcuffed by the police and us walking safely out of here.'

Eventually it was Red Roger himself who put them in touch with the police. He made Simon speak to Inspector Larkman on his mobile phone to prove that they were still alive. With Red Roger breathing in his face, Simon gave the message he had been ordered to deliver.

'Please tell Piers that we'll only be released if he stops animal testing in Andecis immediately. This decision is to be announced in the newspapers and on television. That's the only way to guarantee our safe return. Carolyn and I are both alive and well, but we won't remain that way if Andecis doesn't comply with this request.'

Simon felt extremely agitated after delivering this message. 'We must find a way out of this as soon as possible,' he said to Carolyn at the next opportunity for a whispered conversation. 'Once Andecis makes an announcement like that it'll be very hard to go back to animal testing. The British public are very much in agreement with Red Roger on that subject. Sometimes I think they'd prefer us to use humans in our laboratories. I don't want to get the company involved in a lot of adverse publicity.'

'I don't want us to die either, let's get our priorities right! We'll have to keep visioning a safe exit from this place,' said Carolyn. 'I am sure an opportunity will suddenly present itself. Let's get back in our higher selves and have faith that we'll escape.'

'What do you think our chances of overpowering him would be?'

'Very low. If he's a psychopath as I think he is, he'll be extremely strong. Can you imagine what he'd do to us if we tried and failed?'

'I guess it's too big a risk to take,' said Simon. 'Our best bet is to keep sending him positive energy by focusing on the soul he must have tucked away behind that unpleasant personality of his. Angela taught me to do the same thing with Piers and it worked a treat.'

'I'll join you in that,' Carolyn said. 'Although I think it's a bit much to compare Piers with this nutter.'

Simon managed a weak chuckle.

Just then Red Roger came back into the room so the conversation had to end.

Simon and Carolyn, hard though they tried to be cheerful, were beginning to find their conditions of captivity insufferable. Forced to sit or lie on the floor, which was covered only by a thin and dirty carpet, they were becoming rather stiff. There was no opportunity to wash, or even to brush their teeth. Red Roger's standards of personal hygiene were somewhat wanting, and he imposed the same ones on his prisoners. At least he was a democratic prison warden, who enjoyed no privileges, apart from using for himself the only chair in the room, which was an old armchair, with springs coming through in places. The room was either dim or dark, with light briefly flooding in only when Red Roger opened the door to enter or leave the kitchen.

He was as good as his word, and allowed them to sit there untied during the daytime. That night, before going to sleep, he tied them up again. The combination of tight ropes round their wrists and ankles, Red Roger's snores and the hard floor made sleep at night almost impossible. They dozed on and off during the day, when Red Roger was awake, but were becoming ever more tired. Simon and Carolyn both prayed hard for their release, or at least for some change in their circumstances.

At last a change did come. Red Roger became very worked up after yet another tense telephone conversation in the kitchen. They could hear him shouting and swearing; he was still shouting when he walked towards them through the kitchen door. 'They are stalling,' he roared. 'Let me tell you what I'm going to do to you if they don't comply with what I've asked in the next twenty-four hours.' At this point he waved a long pointed knife at them. It put them in mind of a sacrificial dagger. He fetched a piece of Spam from the kitchen and shredded it on a plate with the knife to show them how sharp it was. Simon imagined that knife cutting through his flesh and shuddered.

'First the woman. I will cut off your lovely tits, my dear, and then I will gouge out those green eyes. As for you, Simon Bruce, you can just imagine what part of *your* anatomy I am going to enjoy cutting off!'

Chapter Sixteen

Simon felt cold sweat break out all over his body. Carolyn slumped beside him. She had fainted. Simon put his arm round her to support her. Red Roger, noting the effect of his words, laughed his horrible laugh. Carolyn soon revived, but her mouth was dry, and she found it hard to swallow. They sat in miserable silence for most of the day, holding hands for comfort. Simon tried to distract himself by thinking of Time Warp and wondering if the regulatory authorities had passed it. Somehow nothing other than staying alive and avoiding mutilation seemed important. 'I'm at least learning one lesson from all of this,' he thought grimly. 'I'll never be frightened by something as trivial as a bollocking from Piers again. This experience really helps to put things into perspective.'

'Keep visualising our safe exit,' Carolyn muttered when Red started to snore that evening.

'You're so brave, Carolyn,' said Simon, giving her a nudge. He couldn't hug her as he wanted to because he was tied up for the night. 'I just keep saying to myself "I can see peace instead of this", over and over again. It does help.'

Red Roger didn't sleep much that night, so Simon and Carolyn had little chance to talk. He seemed to have a tummy bug. They could hear him being sick in the loo. There was also evidence in the lavatory, which he almost never flushed, of a bad case of diarrhoea. He looked very sorry for himself the next day.

'You'll have to fix your own sandwiches today,' he said at around noon, and indicated that Carolyn was to follow him into the kitchen. She was just about to decline, saying that they were not very hungry, when she realised she could use the opportunity to investigate a means of escape. She made the sandwiches, trying hard not to shake, with Red Roger's knife in her back.

When she looked out of the kitchen window, she had to suppress a gasp of surprise at what she saw. Then Red Roger steered her back into the room and locked the kitchen door behind them, putting the key into his pocket. He was erratic with the key. Sometimes he left it in the lock, and then would jump up and retrieve it. Sometimes he put it on the table beside his chair. He always put it in his pocket when he went to the loo.

Later that day Red Roger fell asleep for a short time, and snored loudly as usual. Carolyn used the opportunity to tell Simon about the view she had seen from the kitchen window. 'I know where we are!' she whispered. 'We're in Wales, near to the Pennyrest Hotel. You know, that farm-house hotel we stayed in on our walking holiday.'

'Are you sure?'

'Positive. Do you remember the day we walked from the farmhouse, and went across the fields and then up into the hills? We passed this cottage. It's the only one for miles around, and we commented on how run-down it was and wondered if anyone could possibly be living here.'

'It's near a wobbly stile, the one I broke the step on!'

'That's the one. We're only five or six miles from the hotel we stayed at.'

Red Roger's snores reached a pinnacle and he woke himself up. Later when he was having a noisy vomiting session in the loo Carolyn noticed that he had left his phone in the room. Before Simon realised what she was doing she had texted a message to her friends Roy and Julia, the owners of the hotel. She asked them to tell the police where they were and said that they were going to try and escape and make their way to the hotel. She also said that it would be unwise for the police to try to enter the cottage as it was likely to put her and Simon's lives in grave danger. She finished, putting the phone back just before Red Roger emerged. Her face was flushed, and Simon looked more than usually agitated, but Red Roger did not seem to notice, preoccupied as he was with his health prob-lems. He had another bad night. Carolyn and Simon managed to get a little more sleep than usual, because he did less snoring. He was no better the next day.

'I'm surprised it's him and not us. He hasn't been eating the Spam,' muttered Carolyn. Red Roger seemed distracted, but had not lost his aggression. He kept reminding them about his plans for mutilating their bodies, and the tension in the room rose. Simon muttered to Carolyn 'I can see peace instead of this' whenever he could, and it helped to calm them somewhat.

Finally, their prayers were answered. Red Roger ran suddenly to the loo, leaving the key to the kitchen door on the table. Simon jumped up, unlocked the door and they both moved quietly into the kitchen. Simon locked the door from the inside and they turned their attention to getting out of the back door. Neither of them believed his story about the guard around the cottage. Miraculously the key to the back door was in the lock. Within seconds they were outside, climbing over the back wall and running through a field towards the sanctuary of the Pennyrest Hotel. They climbed over the broken-down stile and ran towards the far end of the next field.

The fresh air felt wonderful. The ground was soggy and wet. It had obviously been raining a lot while they were in captivity; Simon could remember hearing it dripping outside much of the time. But today it was bright and sunny, although cold. They ran as fast as they could. Neither was under any illusion that Red Roger would lose much time in breaking down the kitchen door and chasing after them with his knife. Simon could feel his heart pounding in his ribcage, but he ran as fast as his slightly weakened legs could take him.

They had been climbing gradually but steadily for the first half of the journey, but as they rounded the corner, halfway up a small hill, they could see the hotel in the valley in the middle distance. 'It's all downhill from here,' gasped Simon. He looked over his shoulder and saw Red Roger some way away running towards them. 'Go faster if you can,' he urged Carolyn.

When Carolyn saw the fear on his face she too looked round and saw their captor. 'Speed!' was all she could manage to say as she forced her tired muscles to work harder.

Eventually they climbed over yet another stile and entered a field with a herd of cattle in the far corner. They ran along beside the barbed wire fence towards a gate at the other end.

Just beyond that gate stood the farmhouse, but it was now obscured by trees. They had to run past a feeding trough on the way to the gate. The cattle by now had started moving towards them.

'They could trample us!' cried Carolyn, putting on yet more speed, but feeling the pain in her calves.

'They'll stop at the feeding trough,' said Simon. 'Don't worry, they're only heading our way because they think we're going to feed them.' But they did not stop at the feeding trough. They were a curious and playful herd of young cattle and when Simon and Carolyn passed the feeding trough the cows kept on coming.

Red Roger had just climbed over the stile into the field. He was gaining on them. The cattle were gaining on them even faster. Simon grabbed Carolyn's hand and they both sprinted for the gate. Simon had a stitch, but he kept running. He judged they would get to the gate just before the cows, but that he would not have time to open and shut it before the herd arrived on the spot. They would have to climb over very quickly.

Just before they reached the gate, Carolyn slipped and fell in the mud. The cows at the front of the herd were a few metres away. Simon did not know where he got the strength from, but he picked Carolyn up, ran with her the remaining few steps and literally threw her over. He then vaulted the gate. As he did so the leading cows had their noses jammed up against the wooden bars, and all stood there looking sad at losing the playmates they had been going to have such fun with, trampling them to death.

'We've got to keep going,' Simon managed to say hoarsely as he pulled Carolyn to her feet. 'Red Roger is right behind us.' His knees were weak and shaky.

They ran along the footpath through the woods, and minutes later the lovely thirteenth-century farmhouse came into view. Today it was transformed. Crowds of well-wishers, journalists, photographers and police swarmed around the grounds of the hotel. Two police vans were parked in the driveway. They looked up at the sky as they ran and saw that the whirring noise they had heard off and on during their flight came from police helicopters. Simon thought about the last time he'd seen a helicopter, on the lawns of his Gloucestershire house, and he couldn't believe that it had only been nine months ago. It felt like nine years. He looked behind; there was no sign of Red Roger. I hope he got trampled by those cows, he thought.

They kept running, just in case, and then there was a great roar of joy and shrieks of delight, and the well-wishers ran up the driveway towards them. The police tried to get them to behave in an orderly fashion, but were outnumbered by the cheering mass. There must have been forty people there.

'I feel like I'm just about to win the marathon in the Olympics,' said Carolyn. She was overwhelmed. Tears poured down her cheeks as she ran into the arms of her stepsons. Simon couldn't believe the size of his welcoming party. Katy had flown in from South America, and stood screaming with joy beside Edward and Emily. It seemed as if the whole Andecis board was present, along with Doug Allen and David Jones. Even Piers had shown up, beaming with delight. He scooped Carolyn into his arms when her stepsons released her. Simon was a bit worried by the large turnout from work until he realised that it was Saturday.

'Daddy, Daddy, you're safe, you're safe!' shouted Edward as he hugged his father. At that moment Simon was embarrassed to feel the tears trickling down his own cheeks.

The police politely stood aside while Carolyn and Simon were embraced by everyone in the welcoming party, including perfect strangers who lived in the area and had heard the news of their whereabouts from Julia and Roy, the owners of the hotel. Finally the police asked everyone to leave so that they could interview the escapees, and then give them a chance to rest.

'When it's over come and stay with me in my hotel in Bristol,' said Piers, giving Carolyn a pleading look. But he did extend his hospitality to Simon as well.

'We'll sort all of that out later,' said Carolyn firmly. 'We must talk to the police while there's still some strength left in us.' The crowd took pity on them, and started to wander away. Simon bade an emotional goodbye to his children, promising to see them very soon.

Carolyn took charge again. 'Please interview us in the hotel,' she said to the police, 'I'm not going anywhere looking like this.' They sat in the sitting room of the hotel and spent what seemed like hours with the police. They learnt that Red Roger had previously been in a mental hospital, and that he was

154

known be very unstable. His small gang of supporters had disapproved of his desire to mutilate and kill Simon and Carolyn. They thought it was pointless and would not achieve anything. Many of those tense phone calls were discussions about whether the kidnap victims should continue to live or not. The supporters had remained in Birmingham, and had definitely not been standing guard around the cottage.

Roy and Julia had only picked up the text message earlier that morning. The police ignored the warning not go to the cottage, and had broken into it a few minutes after Red Roger had finally managed to get out of the back door. They could just seen him climbing over the broken stile. The police in the helicopters had watched the whole chase. When Red Roger got to the herd of cattle that had so nearly trampled Simon and Carolyn, he had simply waved his arms and shouted at them, and they had moved away. Carolyn laughed, remembering their terror, and Simon felt a bit foolish.

'Never mind, darling. You are my hero and I'll always remember that you saved my life,' she told him.

'Red Roger does have a way of eliciting obedience,' said Simon with a chuckle.

'The cattle would've trampled you at that stage,' said a kindly policewoman. 'They were moving fast and even Red Roger could not have stopped them then. When he ran up to them they'd come to a halt.'

Simon felt much more kindly disposed towards the police after that. Red Roger had of course been captured, just as he got past the cows. He stood little chance with the helicopters overhead and so many police in the area. He put up no resistance, but vomited all over his captor's feet. The kidnapping had been in all the news media. Simon's colleagues had been interviewed, and so had his mother. 'He was always a disobedient child,' she said on the BBC news. 'I'm not surprised that he didn't tell the police about Red Roger's last warning.'

When the police left, Simon and Carolyn suddenly felt very tired. Julia and Roy gave them towels and clean clothes, and insisted that they stay in the hotel and rest, for as long as they liked. Simon and Carolyn accepted gratefully, having only enough energy left in them to walk up the stairs to the bedrooms. They walked first into Simon's huge room overlooking the woods they had only recently run through, and stood there for a long time facing each other. Simon looked at Carolyn. She was covered in mud, her hair a mass of blond spikes with the dark roots beginning to show. Her face was striped. The tears had trickled down through grime leaving pale streaks. Her skin was greasy and spotty with tiny cuts in places. Nevertheless Simon knew that he wanted her and no one else. He realised that Piers would always be in the background wanting to take her back, but after all, you don't get value without taking calculated risks. He took courage from his motto.

Gently, he took her in his arms. 'I love you, Carolyn. I want you to be mine forever and I won't take no for an answer.'

'It must really be true love,' she said happily, catching sight of herself in the mirror. 'I want you too, but I want a bath even more.'

Half an hour later, they rendezvoused in Simon's bedroom, both now squeaky clean, and no longer smelling of sweat and dirty lavatories. They got into bed and found that they had enough energy left to make love. It was slow, passionate and indescribably sweet. Afterwards they fell into a deep sleep and did not wake up until the next morning.

'If you had snored,' said Carolyn, 'I would have killed you.'

'Another close shave. Life is very precarious at present.' Simon held Carolyn in his arms and stroked her. 'I feel as if I have been looking for you all of my life, and now I've come home. I'm as happy as I ever remember being.'

Carolyn purred like a kitten. 'What a wonderful end to our adventure.' She looked into his dark brown eyes, saw the depth of feeling in there and felt the same thrill she had felt on the train going to Paris.

Simon's stomach growled with hunger. 'I'm ravenous, it must be time for a Spam sandwich.'

At that moment Julia walked in with a full English breakfast on a tray. She discreetly failed to mention that Carolyn was in Simon's bed, and not in her own. When she had gone they ate six little bananas between them before tackling the bacon, eggs, sausages, mushrooms, tomatoes and black pudding. Next they ate the toast and marmalade. After the feast they enjoyed reading about their run and rescue in the *Sunday Times*, which Julia had brought with the breakfast.

'What shall we do now?' asked Carolyn, with an inviting smile on her face.

Simon turned towards her, and, pulling the bedclothes

back, gazed at her lovely body. He felt his passion take him over. 'Let me show you.' Simon put the tray on the floor, pulled her towards him, and made love to her again. It was even better than the night before. They fell asleep again afterwards.

When they woke up it was raining hard. They looked through the window at the wet, grey world outside and Carolyn said, 'I don't think I ever want to get up.'

'Then don't,' said Simon, and they lay there until Julia brought their lunch. In total they spent twenty-four hours in bed. Roy and Julia kept bringing them the most delicious meals, with salads and fruit which tasted as if they had come from the Garden of Eden. Mercifully there was no telephone in the bedroom. Roy and Julia fielded all their calls, which were mostly from journalists and from Piers. Everyone was told very firmly that they were sleeping and not to be disturbed. No one was allowed into the hotel, apart from the other guests. Once when the sun came out briefly they considered going for a walk to Red Roger's cottage, but decided against it. They did not think they would cope if the tins of Spam were still stacked up in the kitchen.

The next day they had another long session with the police in Cardiff. They provided detailed evidence of Red Roger's threats and treatment of them in the cottage. It was formal and stressful, bringing back some extremely unpleasant memories. However they could understand the importance of what they were doing. They would be key witnesses at Red Roger's trial, when it came up. The police hoped that they would be able to put him away, probably in a secure psychiatric hospital, for a long time.

When they got back to the hotel Julia gave them an e-mail which she had printed off. It was an invitation to a celebration party held by Andecis at the Ritz the next evening. Piers had added on the bottom, 'This is a command invitation.'

Simon and Carolyn looked at each other. 'I guess we'd better go,' they said in unison, before going back to bed to gather their strength.

A limousine called to collect them from the hotel the next morning. When they arrived in London, Carolyn was taken to her mews house in South Kensington first. Simon escorted her into the house, and then got back into the limousine and headed towards Holland Park. This was the first time in many days he had been parted from Carolyn. He felt strangely bereft.

In the early evening he collected her in his car, which had somehow been delivered to his house, and they walked into the Ritz together. The room exploded in cheers as they entered. Champagne corks popped, and music began to play. Everyone who could get near to them hugged Simon, kissed Carolyn, and welcomed them back to freedom. Piers came over, put his arms round both of them and said, 'Actually, this party is not just for you, although you are the guests of honour. We're also celebrating the acceptance of Time Warp by the regulators.'

Simon and Carolyn looked at each other with guilty expressions on both faces. They had completely forgotten about the drug. 'Three cheers for Time Warp,' shouted Simon. He jumped up on to the platform in front of the band, pulling Carolyn with him, and they did a celebratory jig, while the room exploded with 'For they are jolly good fellows'. Verity collared him after that and told him how worried they had all been for his safety, and Carolyn's.

'The media made Red Roger out to be a really dangerous man.'

'He was, but also rather pathetic.'

'Simon, I want you to know that although I was worried, I wasn't pessimistic. I felt sure that you would come through. When the police told Piers where you were he called each of us to say he was going to the Pennyrest Hotel and we all decided to go with him. We made it into work, early on Saturday morning though it was, crowded into his stretch limousine and roared down the motorway. And when the two of you burst out of the woods like two muddy goblins I was overjoyed.'

For the second time that week Simon felt the tears welling at the back of his eyes. Overflowing with emotion he changed the subject and took Verity over to the buffet table for some food.

The rest of the evening was a blur. He vaguely remembered seeing Carolyn and Piers having an intense conversation. Shortly afterwards Carolyn came over and asked if she could spend the night with Simon. 'Yes, if you promise not to keep me awake with too many demands on my body,' he remembered drunkenly saying. They left his car at the Ritz and got a taxi home; neither of them was sober enough to drive.

Chapter Seventeen

Piers and Simon sat facing each other in Simon's Mayfair office. On the surface their conversation looked like a normal exchange between two executives. Piers had dropped in to see him on his way to the airport following a routine visit to the London head office of Andecis. But under the surface lurked an air of challenge and competition. It was the first real test of Simon's newfound confidence with Piers following his kidnapping adventure. After congratulating him on his successes of the last few months, Piers came to the point.

'I understand that you and Carolyn are lovers?'

Simon nodded and waited.

'I'm sorry that Red Roger didn't kill you back there on your tea break holiday in that cottage in Wales.' Simon knew that Piers, as usual, was exaggerating to make a point, but he could hear the strain in his voice. 'On the other hand, perhaps it's better that he didn't. You're making us all a lot of money at the moment.'

That was a reference to the steady climb of the Andecis share price since October. The recovering strength of the stock market was helping, of course, but Andecis had bene-fited enormously from the publicity surrounding the happy ending to the kidnapping. It was a fortunate coincidence that Time Warp had been approved at the same time. The Andecis success story with their first blockbuster drug since the merger, the heroic behaviour of two of their leading execu-tives, and the company's mission to transform and open up the lives of older people, all hit the headlines at the same time. Simon had ruthlessly exploited his press exposure to tell the world about Andecis and its plans.

He thought now about that mission and felt strength flood through him. He was not afraid of Piers; Red Roger had put that relationship into perspective for him. He continued to stay silent and look expectant, remaining in his higher self.

'I thought I asked you to look after her. Now I find that although you are happy to share her bed, you haven't the decency to make an honest woman of her. In fact you're not even living together!'

Simon smiled. This was a pretty ironic confrontation coming from Piers. He kept his silence a little longer while he considered his options. He could get back into his control drama and expend a lot of energy defensively explaining that it was Carolyn who insisted on being a live-out lover. He could play aloof, and tell Piers that it was none of his business. He could let his aggression push him into counter-intimidator and tell Piers that this was the pot calling the kettle black. Simon chose none of the above. Instead he stayed in his higher self and asked for inspiration, which duly came. Suddenly he saw Piers not as the menacing enemy, but as a man suffering from divided loyalties and the consequent loss of a relationship he treasured. He also remembered that this man was a gift to him, to help him to work through his fears, and leave them behind.

'Piers, I know you care very deeply for Carolyn's well-being. I also know that you are a very significant person in her life, and that if circumstances had been different, the two of you would still be together. I'd like you to know that I treasure her as much as you do, and would cheerfully die for her. Carolyn is in a very good place right now. She's finding herself, and needs to maintain at least some independence to do that. It's a privilege to be close to her and to see this emerging maturity and grace. She's giving tremendous leadership to her team, and to the marketing function globally. I'm always there for her, but she doesn't need that much looking after these days; she is pretty strong.'

It was Piers's turn to be silent. He sat stroking his chin for a while. Finally he said, 'I have to go now. Maybe you are the best thing for Carolyn after all. I want the best for her, so make sure you are always that.'

Simon left the office at the same time as Piers. He had a meeting with Angela, and decided to walk to her office in St James's rather than take a taxi. As he covered the short distance he savoured the weak winter sunshine. It was late February: a year since they had started working together. He planned to renew their contract for another year, as her help had been invaluable. Their coaching sessions had changed over time. At first Angela had given him a lot of teaching and guidance. Then as Simon started to incorporate his new philosophy into his whole life he'd noticed a subtle change. He still came to the meetings with questions and conundrums, but now he was the one who was coming up with the answers. Angela was his sounding board, rather than his mentor.

'Let's talk about Piers,' Simon suggested as he sat down facing her.

'That'll make a change.'

'Not fair. He hasn't been on my mind for some time.'

'OK. It's true we haven't discussed him for ages. I was taking a longer historical perspective. In fact, I was beginning to think Piers was no longer a problem for you.'

'He isn't normally. Every now and again he lobs a grenade into the conversation, as he did just now. But I seem able to catch it and toss it away to safety before it causes harm. I'm still slightly wary of him, but also very grateful to him for the lessons he's helped me to learn. I don't think I do control dramas with anyone now.'

'Are you familiar with Carl Jung's concept of the shadow?'

'Yes, vaguely.'

'Jung's view is that it's necessary to have a shadow, since we cannot be everything that it would be possible for us to be. We choose which aspects of ourselves to show to the world through our personalities. If we fool ourselves that we're all sweetness and light, then our aggressive, horrid shadow will appear in our lives in the form of other people, like Piers and Serena. It also shows up in our dreams, and in our behaviour when we're stressed.'

'So it's all back to accepting the fact that I'm human, and have this shadow side, and remembering to forgive myself and everyone else? Let me start by defending Piers: he is still sometimes aggressive, but no longer horrid. He never humiliates me in public any more, and is mostly quite supportive.'

'That's good. You've created that improved reality for yourself. You've worked hard at accepting and loving Piers, and at increasing your own self-love. The result is that you invite more caring loving people into your life.'

161

'Apart from Red Roger, that is.'

'Do you want to talk about what happened?'

'You bet I do. It was the most amazing experience of my life. Not one I want to repeat, but quite character-forming.'

'What lessons did you learn from it?'

'First of all I would like to tell you what lessons I put into it. My efforts to send positive energy to both Serena and Piers trained me for this event. My lessons from you about staying in my higher self also helped. Carolyn and I were both able to use these concepts to keep us sane, and also probably to keep Red Roger from mutilating us before he got sick. I was scared all right, but I managed to pull myself out of the valleys every time and get back up there with my positive expectations of escape. I'm sure that saved our lives.'

'It probably did. You were both very brave.' Angela poured Simon a cup of coffee, smiling fondly at him.

'The lesson I've learnt is to put all other fears into perspective. Once you face death, no other fear is worth worrying about. I wish I could have learnt this before, then I wouldn't have had to go through that frightful kidnapping. So ironically, as a result of having that dreadful experience, I'm now very much at peace. Who was it that said: "Man's mind stretched to a new idea never goes back to its original dimensions"?'

'Oliver Wendell Holmes.'

'So if you think I look relaxed, it's because I finally know just who I am and what I'm capable of, and am happy with that.'

Angela was impressed by the Simon who now sat in front of her, and said so. They then decided to review progress over the last year. Angela believed in celebrating success, and in being grateful for it. Simon would previously have marred his enjoyment of it by grinding away in his mind about the things that were not yet right, and the future threats and uncertainties. Today he was getting better at letting go of the outcome, and seeing setbacks as learning opportunities.

'We've put one big new drug on to the market, which thanks to Red Roger got more publicity than any other drug in the history of this country. Rondina is looking good for May, and Evereadiness is targeted for September. We hope that Persen, the drug for prostate cancer, and Newear, the drug for deafness, will be ready for the regulators late next year. Two major drugs a year is good going for a drug company of our size. We're a significant player, but not yet a giant.'

'Are you confident that those drugs will be successful?'

'They're all looking very good. Delster has strengthened our research capacity considerably, and since the leadership development programme got going we have had no cause to be nervous about losing any of our research teams. Cultural integration is still a problem, but we are cascading the message abut taking the best from both cultures throughout the organisation on the leadership programmes. Some very sound ideas are coming back up to us from the layer below the board, and we're paying attention to them, and acknowledging their source.

'Mike and Eric are both doing a lot better, thanks to you and Malcolm Manners I'm sure. As Mike reined in his tendency to bully, Eric began to make fewer of those gross errors of judgement. The rest of Mike's senior team seem to be basking in the improved atmosphere. The commercial implications of this breakthrough are good for us, as you can imagine.

'Four of the Zeus senior people have left. They were unhappy anyway at not being on the European, or even on the UK, board. The straw that broke the camel's back for them was the leadership programme and the assessments preceding it. As you said, there would be some laggards when we started that programme and those who could not change would leave or be fired. Thankfully we didn't have to fire them, as they left of their own accord. We may lose some more, but I'll have to take that in my stride.'

'As long as it's not Doug Allen!'

'Isn't that a turnaround? Last summer we were trying to decide whether or not to replace him. Now his department is giving the support the research teams need, and he has finally completed his architecture integration, with a leading-edge solution which he claims will transform IT in Andecis worldwide.'

Simon was cautiously optimistic. If it worked they would be miles out ahead of the competition, even the giant drug companies. However he had been around long enough to view the term leading-edge with some cynicism. It normally meant leading to an early grave with panics, breakdowns and delays. Nonetheless he kept up his positive visions of success, and gave an interim pay rise to the new IT operations manager, who was proving to be worth his weight in gold.

'The leadership development programme's been going for around six months now. What sort of impact is it making?' asked Angela.

'The response from the managers is pretty good; there's some cynicism, but mostly they're finding it inspirational. We continue to enjoy staff retention rates above the industry norm. I've noticed that my team, who've all had coaches since the autumn, are much more open to change. In fact they are much more open full stop. I think Piers, who as you know only turns up every two months, and didn't participate in the leadership programme, finds the openness disconcerting. He goes for the jugular with my directors sometimes, and they just stay calm and agree. If he's being unfair, then usually someone else speaks up in the victim's defence. I shouldn't say victim; there are no victims on our board any more. That's such a change. We all used to be victims in the past when Piers went on the rampage.'

Angela looked pleased. 'How are you doing with your efforts to win sponsors other than Piers?'

'Now that I'm sharing the leadership effort for the mission with the rest of the European team, I've created the time to go to New York every two months. My visits are short, but I make sure that they all know what we're up to. With a little help from my senior US sponsors I've managed to persuade Tony Albertino to start a programme similar to our leadership transformation programme. Having sponsors other than Piers has been critical in achieving this. Piers can see the commercial results of our change in culture in Europe, but he's uncomfortable living with it. It doesn't suit his style. He wants us to go ahead with it, but he doesn't make a good advocate. I'm not sure if he really understands what's behind it all, although I've explained it to him as best I can.'

Simon chuckled to himself, thinking how nice it was to turn the tables on Piers for a change. When the new vision, mission and culture were being discussed it was Piers who fidgeted in his chair and sometimes found himself searching for words.

'The IT architecture breakthrough is giving me a lot of visibility over there. They took a gamble when they gave the British team responsibility for that task worldwide. Doug was seen at the start as having the brains and the ideas, but not the organising capabilities. It was I who championed him, so I have to take full responsibility for his success or failure. Interestingly, my job will be on the line if that architecture integration is a damp squib. They probably wouldn't sack me, but I would lose credibility and sponsorship to the point where it would be hard for me to continue taking the mission forward. I would have to resign.'

'Are you losing sleep over this?' asked Angela, although she had a pretty good idea what the answer would be.

'No. I have faith that I'll achieve my mission, even if it's not in Andecis. I no longer worry unduly about my status, my income or my security. I have the impression that the universe is behind me, or to be more precise behind my mission.'

'If you did have to leave Andecis, what do you think would happen to you?'

'I imagine I would get another job, probably with one of the pharmaceutical giants.'

'What's your profile like in the pharmaceutical world outside Andecis?'

'Everyone knows of me – the kidnapping put me and the company on the map.'

'Yes, you're well known as a good chief executive who has masterminded two successful mergers. However if Doug failed you, you'd be no different in their eyes to a number of other executives with a list of successes and setbacks to their name. I think there's more to you than that. Your mission, your beliefs, your inspirational style of leadership and your courage mark you out as a transformational leader. Don't hide your light under a bushel. You want to make sure you're not stopped in your tracks towards your mission because a short-term setback costs you your job, and the market doesn't fully know your worth.'

'Angela, those remarks coincide with a germinating idea of mine that I should get started on an international programme to tell the world about the impact of transformational leadership on our company. This'll give me the profile I need outside Andecis, and spread an important message at the same time. I'll get going on this programme.

As usual, when I do things that take my mission forward, I benefit my own career as well.'

When he left Angela picked up the phone and called her husband. 'How about a late lunch?' she asked. 'I have something to celebrate.'

'So, what's this all about?' Geoff looked at her curiously as she sipped her wine at their table in the Caprice. He had never seen Angela drink at lunchtime before, except at weddings and christenings.

'It's Simon, my favourite client. He's on his way to the moon. I really feel I've made a difference to his life.'

'Well, I'll drink to that,' said Geoff. 'In fact why don't we get quietly drunk together and then stagger home to bed?'

An attractive pink colour flooded into Angela's cheeks. 'I think you're taking advantage of my good mood. Besides, the two little ones will be at home with the nanny.'

'We'll tell them to go to the cinema.'

'Oh all right then, I give in,' she giggled, and finished her wine.

One year later

Simon and Carolyn sat on their hotel-room balcony overlooking the city of Aqaba on the Red Sea. They were nearing the end of a ten-day walking holiday in Jordan. In the last year they had seen Andecis go from strength to strength. Both Rondina and Evereadiness were accepted by the regulators, and were being marketed successfully. After such giant strides, they felt they deserved a holiday. They visited Petra, walked in the mountains and in the desert, rode camels, admired the desert sky at night, and ate wonderful feasts in Bedouin camps. Now they were drinking Pimms on their balcony and enjoying the sunset over Aqaba. They had walked in the desert all day, and the Mövenpick hotel in Aqaba seemed like an oasis, but an oasis with hot showers and swimming pools.

They had been happy together for a year and a half. They still maintained separate houses, but spent all of their free time together. Theirs was a non-demanding relationship. Carolyn gave Simon no instructions or criticisms either in bed or out of bed. They quickly forgave each other for the little and big lapses that human beings make from time to

166

time. Their only fight had been over Piers, and it had happened quite recently. One weekend Simon was at Carolyn's house when the phone rang. Thinking that she had not yet returned from her run in the park, he picked up the phone. As he did so he heard Piers saying hello to Carolyn. He just could not bring himself to put the receiver down. Piers wanted to know if Carolyn was well and happy. They swapped news and banter for a while, and then Piers said, 'Why don't we get back together again?' Simon waited with interest to hear Carolyn's answer.

'You know my terms.' That ended the conversation. Piers sighed and said goodbye. Simon was still holding the receiver in his hand and thinking about Carolyn's answer when she walked into the room.

'Caught you red-handed,' she said with an annoyed look on her face.

'Carolyn, believe me, I picked it up thinking you weren't yet back.'

'Then why didn't you put it down straight away? I don't listen in to your phone calls, or pry in any way.'

Caught off guard as he was, instinct made him counter-attack and he said, 'I don't have an ex-lover in the background who wants me to come back to her. And besides, what would you do if he did offer to meet your terms?'

'I don't know the answer, but it's not an issue. You know as well as I do that he'll never meet them. You and I planned that strategy together, sitting on the mountaintops in Wales. What bothers me is the lack of trust behind the eavesdropping.'

Simon realised at that moment it was fate he was refusing to trust, not just Carolyn. 'Forgive me please, my love. It was a breach of trust. I don't know what made me hold on to that receiver, you know it's not how I normally operate.'

That was the end of it. Carolyn, who did not bear grudges, never mentioned it again. Even so, Simon kicked himself over it for a few days.

'Every day I make so many decisions not to take impetuous actions in the first rush of anger or anxiety, but to see it from the other person's point of view first. Why was I not able to do that with Carolyn, who is so important to me?' he asked Angela. 'I guess hearing Piers's voice triggered a descent into my lower self, and when down there fear made me want to check out her loyalty.'

167

Angela didn't need to add much to that discussion as she could see that Simon had worked out the answer for himself. She just helped him to forgive himself for being human, as Carolyn had done days ago. When back in his higher self he remembered he was the creator of the reality he was enjoying with Carolyn, and that it was far better to be grateful for such a wonderful lover than to waste energy worrying that he would lose her one day.

They both had full diaries, and travelled far too much. Simon was busy spreading the word about transformational leadership internationally. Carolyn had spent the year visiting Andecis offices all over the world, getting them to join in her programme to take drug and other useful information to the end customer. Every region required a different way to achieve these objectives, depending on the local culture, laws and institutions, so it provided a fascinating political, history and geography lesson for Carolyn.

Sometimes she and Simon found themselves able to travel together, but often they were like ships passing in the night. This did not deter them. They enjoyed each other's company when they were together, and made a point of having frequent short holidays together. They had climbed Mount Kilimanjaro, visited the Galapagos, swum with the Great White sharks in Cape Town, and now they had come to the end of another wonderful vacation.

It had been a very good year for the company. The IT integration programme had achieved spectacular results. Although there were teething problems, Andecis was now out ahead in the drug company world thanks to the speed and accuracy of their technology processing. Simon had most definitely not lost his job. Headhunters called him frequently with attractive-sounding offers. He politely listened to them all, but none promised the challenge and fulfilment he got from taking his mission forward in Andecis.

Piers had recently suffered a heart attack. He was back at work now, having in true Piers fashion thrown himself wholeheartedly into his rehabilitation programme. His recovery was quick and complete, but he was a mellowed man. His brain, and therefore his challenges, were just as sharp, but he put a stop to his gruelling schedule of international travel. He encouraged Simon and Tony Albertino to do much of the travelling for him. This suited Simon, as it enabled him to kill two birds with one stone, spreading the word about his mission, and doing company business. His profile both inside and outside Andecis was high.

'Let's celebrate Andecis' successes of the last year,' he said, raising his glass of Pimms, as they relaxed on the balcony. 'Angela has taught me to always be grateful for the good things in life.'

'Cheers,' said Carolyn. 'This has been a spectacular year. It's also been lovely for me to watch your transformation over the last two years. You're no longer the tough, swashbuckling but frightened chief executive I comforted the morning the Grace Lee scandal hit the papers.'

'You've seen me at my worst.' Simon grinned, remembering those days. 'I was such a prick, with my big country house, lord of the manor lifestyle and my demanding mistresses. All those things ever gave me was anxiety that I would lose them.'

'You did lose them, but it seemed to make you happier. You are a changed man now.'

'As soon a I let go of my need to protect my gains, I started to get all I really needed. That was success for the company, progress for our mission, a totally loyal team, the love of my children, and you. Although I must admit the universe did rather put me through the hoops to win you.'

'I was falling in love with you even before the kidnapping. You didn't need to bring Red Roger into our lives to get me to go to bed with you.'

'Now you tell me!'

'Anyway, I'm sure it was life-changing for both of us. To go back to your transformation, it has been wonderful to watch you gain such moral authority. I'm so lucky to be close to you.'

'I'm not good all of the time, I have my lapses,' said Simon, feeling ridiculously pleased at Carolyn's remarks. 'It's the change in my beliefs that's changed me. I think now that whenever I reach out to the world, my driving forces are love, hope, joy, trust and empowerment. These things are always in the back of my mind. I want to help people to discover their own power and capability to love and respect themselves.'

'Well, it shows, darling. And yet it doesn't detract from your business leadership in any way. I suppose it's the authentic power that has replaced your reliance on external power.'

'I discovered some time ago that authentic power is the only sort you can hang on to. External power comes and goes and only brings stress and anxiety.' Simon decided that he'd received enough accolades for the time being. 'I wonder if you realise just how much of my inspiration comes from you, Carolyn? Many of the things you're complimenting me on are qualities I saw in you when I first got to know you in Paris. I can remember you saying that your mission was to make life better for the people with whom you're in contact. I've watched you do this with your coaching and your wonderfully subtle communication skills. Your marketing teams are the most creative and impressive of any in our industry. And best of all you've certainly made life better for me.'

'I think we'd better disband this mutual admiration society or our heads will be so big we won't get through the door.'

They lapsed into companionable silence and watched the lights twinkling in the city of Aqaba as dark fell. They could see the remnants of the sunset in the sky to the west, and could just make out the outlines of the graceful palms in the fading light. Up in the desert sky the stars were brighter than the lights of the city. It was as if they were in a fish bowl, but swimming in twinkling lights rather than water. As they finished their drinks Simon ruminated on the contrast between this relationship and the previous one, the short-lived affair with Serena. So many couples spend so much time getting each other to shape up, he thought to himself. Yet here we are, embarrassing each other with praise. I'm a lucky man.

Simon was planning to ask Carolyn to marry him. He had not broached the subject before, as he was very keen to respect her need for independence. However he had now come to the conclusion that there was no need for them to have a conventional marriage. They could carry on as they were, living in separate houses, if that suited her. It wasn't as if they were trying to raise a family. What counted was the love and trust between them, and time apart did nothing to threaten that.

The next day they swam in all three of the hotel's swimming pools, and in the sea. They agreed that the sea was too salty and that they preferred the pools. In the afternoon, while Carolyn was having a sleep, Simon went out into the town and bought a diamond engagement ring from a jewellery shop, which had been particularly recommended to him by a Jordanian friend. He put the ring in its box in his jacket pocket, and went down with Carolyn to eat dinner on the restaurant patio in the warm tropical night. Several of the other members of their walking group joined them at their table for dinner, so he decided to wait until later in the evening to propose to her. After dinner, Simon suggested to Carolyn that they go back to their room for a nightcap on the balcony. When they got upstairs Simon held the bedroom door open with one hand and fingered the ring box with the other. He was looking forward to seeing Carolyn's eyes widen with surprise when he looked down at the floor; an envelope containing a message was lying there. It was from Piers. Simon read it to Carolyn.

'Get the hell over here, both of you! Tantron Pine want to buy us. I can't handle this on my own.'

'Tantron Pine!' gasped Carolyn, her eyes wide with surprise but not for the reason Simon had been anticipating. 'They're the biggest pharmaceutical company in the world now. We must phone Piers right away. He's in New York so he'll still be at the office.'

They contacted Piers, and Simon got caught up in the excitement, forgetting about the ring. Joining up with Tantron Pine would give them an unassailable position in the market. They would then be big enough to influence governments to collaborate with their programmes to improve life for older people. Simon knew that this merger had to go through. It was an answer to Andecis' strategic goals; he saw his mission going forward and had a sleepless night anticipating all that was to follow. Carolyn also tossed and turned for the same reason.

The next day they flew back to London, and slept most of the way on the aeroplane, recharging their batteries for what lay ahead. Simon still had the ring in his jacket pocket, but he realised that he might have to wait quite a while before an appropriate moment for slipping it on to Carolyn's finger came around again.

Chapter Eighteen

When the time came to tell the European board of Andecis' interest in Tantron Pine's offer, there was bedlam in the boardroom. Carolyn, Roger and Peter already knew about the deal, but the others had a lot to say.

'What about the mission? Have you given up on that?'

'I know we'll all be rich if this goes through, but are we letting them buy us out of our values?'

'We have worked so hard on our culture, and it's brought us success. If we sell to one of the giants, they will break us up and soon there'll be nothing left of what we treasure.'

Most of the reactions followed along those lines. Piers and Simon did their best to explain that, although it was a risk, the hoped-for outcome was that being part of such a large company would propel them further and faster towards their mission. 'Tantron Pine have leverage in the markets and with governments that we can only dream about,' said Piers.

Finally Simon said, 'This is our mission, not just mine, or Piers's. Bring all of your concerns to us and we'll negotiate like mad. But please keep your sights on our corporate strategy to grow to a point where we supply two per cent of the market. With Tantron Pine we'll be in that position. We've been successful in phase one of our journey to our mission. As a result a high-quality purchaser is interested. Now we have to hold our breaths and move into phase two. I see this merger as a godsend in propelling us into the sort of league that will ensure sustained success. You know that we cannot give you cast-iron guarantees, but as I've always said, you don't create value without taking risks. We have a dream that we've dreamt together, and now together we've pulled this opportunity into our lives. Let's make it work, not reject it out of hand.'

He sensed a lot of anxiety still in the room. They'll have to live with that, he thought to himself. But maybe I can say a few words to help them to keep it to a manageable level.

'I share your fears. I feel them myself. To take our mission forward we now face a challenge which will bring growth and change, and it is normal to be worried in the face of the unknown.'

Carolyn joined in at this point. 'You know, we're going to have to face mergers and change, whether we do so with Tantron Pine or some other company. The upside of Tantron Pine is that they are an impressive organisation, with high-quality products, mature management and infrastructure, and they're huge. That gives them the leverage Piers spoke about. The downside is that we don't know if a giant like this will just gobble us up like you fear, take the bits they want, and leave no sign of the precious culture we've developed. We have to face this fear squarely. But however we grow, we'll confront change and uncertainty, and grow we must, to progress our mission.'

Simon continued after casting a grateful glance at Carolyn. 'Our mission propels us to grow, and that inevitably brings fear. Carolyn, and all of you today, have articulated the form it will take. However I think that the issue is fear itself.'

At this point Piers began to look distinctly uncomfortable, but did not interrupt.

'When we choose to grow as human beings, and that's the core of this immediate challenge, we have to learn to enjoy our fear. People perform best when they're moderately anxious anyway. Remember that fear comes from our illusion of separateness. It comes from forgetting that we create our own reality. Nothing is written on tablets of stone. Our whole world is about change and uncertainty. I ask you to acknowledge your fears, then rejoin me in that vision of building a company that can transform old age for millions of people.'

Piers got up and helped himself to a cup of coffee, then sat back down again. He opened his mouth to join in the discussion, but thought better of it and kept quiet, looking slightly bemused. This was not the sort of debate he was accustomed to having at board meetings.

'Everything we thought was solid and predictable is now up for grabs, it seems to me,' said Peter.

'That's right,' Simon continued. 'Old structures are being challenged, former certainty gives way to doubt, and that's both worrying and confusing. Hold on to your dreams, and Piers and I will fight to hold on to our heritage. We will pull out if it seems hopeless, although my intuition tells me that this deal is promising for us. As you keep your vision in the forefront of your mind, remember to let go of the outcome. Something new and good will emerge from this shake-up, but we don't know the exact form or timing right now.'

Simon was as good as his word. He took all concerns seriously, answering those he could himself, and getting answers from Tantron Pine or negotiating with them over the rest. He also made sure that Tony Albertino and Piers helped him to do the same across the world.

At first the negotiations with the Tantron Pine top team were tough. Piers had most of the contact with Adam Falls, the chief executive of Tantron Pine. Simon had to deal with the nitty-gritty details of the financial deal, the structure of the merged companies, and the budgets for important activities and programmes. At first the Tantron Pine team saw him as a pushover. The goodness that shone from him, the calm respectful way he dealt with them, struck them as weakness. But as time went on their view changed. Simon stuck to his guns. He had a mission to defend. He accepted no vague promises, and insisted on everything important being written into the contract. Eventually they negotiated their way through everything except the main sticking points. These were the relative independence of Andecis, and the budgets to ensure the continuation of the leadership development and marketing programmes worldwide.

'We achieved commercial success because we are a learning organisation,' Simon told them. 'We're committed to the continued education of our employees and of our customers. I have no fall-back position on this. For the deal to go through I must be guaranteed budgets for at least five years.'

On the independence of Andecis he did have a fall-back position, which was phased integration with Tantron Pine after five years of independence. His bottom line was two years of independence, but of course he didn't mention this.

Enrico Gultosi, the financial director of Tantron Pine, was his toughest protagonist. He was old-school, arrogant, pompous and the worst listener possible. He could not understand, or chose not to hear, Simon's articulate arguments about the commercial strengths of the Andecis culture. Simon kept his team informed of developments, and while they cheered him on over every success, they kept up the pressure over preserving that culture. Enrico wanted the two companies to integrate fully, to rationalise, and to enjoy the fruits of economies of scale, but Simon's team did not want to disappear as an entity. They saw no hope for their mission and culture down that path.

Enrico sat with Simon in the armchairs in his office, after a frustrating afternoon of negotiation which had achieved nothing but stalemate. 'I will not be here for a couple of weeks,' he said. 'I am going to the Dolomites, where my family have a holiday home in the mountains. We are also going to see *Aida* at Verona. Next week will be the last chance to go to the opera at the amphitheatre this season.'

'How wonderful. I went to *Carmen* at Verona a few years ago and found it the musical experience of a lifetime.'

Enrico's lips twisted into something between a smile and a sneer. 'It's a shame that so many tourists come to the opera there. They have no appreciation of the musical traditions and history of our country. My family go back to the fifteenth century and are distantly related to the Borgias ...'

Enrico continued to boast about his family and their traditions, but Simon had stopped listening. He suddenly had a mental picture of Enrico the warrior prince, dressed in the garb of his Renaissance ancestor, scheming, poisoning and slashing enemies with his sword. It gave him an insight into the dangerous world Enrico still felt that he lived in, five hundred years later.

'It's no wonder I can't get through to him,' he said to Carolyn later that evening as he lay on his blue sofa with his head on her lap. 'And to make matters worse, after putting up with him all afternoon, I was collared by Verity as soon as he left. She really let me have it about breaking up the company.'

'It's an anxious time for everyone. You must be under constant pressure. Ironically the anxiety of your team members stems from their loyalty to you, and to the mission.'

'Hoist by my own petard.'

'Remember what's really important is that you don't make crucial decisions when you're angry, frustrated or tired. You only want to do that when you're able to listen to your intuition.'

Simon saw Angela the next day and continued the discussion with her.

'I never thought it was going to be easy, but the pressure is high and mounting.'

'You know if you find yourself forcing, struggling and overworking to make things happen, you're not following the path of your intuition. There are no right or wrong decisions. Each choice you make will bring rich opportunities for experiencing new angles on life. You learn a different set of lessons from each path. But, on the other hand, you might as well seek out the path that takes your forward in the most enjoyable and rewarding way. That'll be the most direct route to your goal.'

'I need some more quiet time to listen to my intuition. I think I'll leave my paperwork behind this weekend and go walking along the South Downs with Carolyn.'

'That's just what you need. I think you're letting the pressure push you down into your lower self, and you're losing touch with the principles of creating reality.'

'What are you thinking of precisely?' asked Simon.

'Remember that the manner of how, when and what you desire shows up is something that you must not try to control. Leave the how and when up to God and the universe, without judging, demanding or insisting upon your prerequisites. Knowing that your dream will be realised is enough. Cultivate the power of patient detachment from the form of the outcome. When you're certain of the outcome, as you've been now for over two years, you can afford to wait without anxiety. Your faith and your patience will put you at ease.'

'As usual, Angela, you've hit the nail on the head. I'll try to relax a bit and let the world turn by itself instead of trying to push it.' Simon walked back to his office with a lighter step.

He went to the South Downs with Carolyn that weekend. They walked along the South Downs Way in silence much of the time, and when they talked it was about anything other than work. The scenery was quietly, beautifully English. They struck good weather and had blue skies for both days. Sheep roamed contentedly in the open pastureland. Before them the landscape of Sussex stretched for miles in the distance, with farms and villages tucked away here and there, looking no different from how they had hundreds of years ago. The paths were as muddy as they had been in the Middle Ages. They tramped down from the South Downs Way, along steep tracks between avenues of overhanging beech trees. The footpath took them through the farms they had seen from the tops of the Downs. They walked in an orchard beside a stream flowing through an old mill. The elderly couple who lived there were gathering apples from the gnarled old trees. Simon and Carolyn fell into conversation with the couple who told them about the flood hazard from the stream, which had swollen with the recent rains. They were given as many apples as they could carry in their backpacks. They found a bench in the village and sat there eating two apples each to lighten the load. It was timelessly peaceful, and Tantron Pine seemed to belong in another world, perhaps in Renaissance Italy with Enrico's warrior ancestors.

They made their way back to the hotel along a footpath that took them through yet more farms and villages. It was getting dark when they came to a gate in a corner of a field with a large band of mud slurry around it. They picked their way carefully through the mud, with their walking boots sinking in deep, so that every step was an effort. Their boots now weighed twice as much as usual, swollen by mud, both inside and out. The effort to pull each foot out of the mud and take a step forward became enormous. Then the inevitable happened, Simon left his boot behind as he tried to lift his foot, lost his balance, and fell face forward. When he picked his face out of the mud Carolyn laughed so hard that she lost her balance and fell down beside him. They both sat there, laughing until they were too weak to get up. 'I'm glad there are no rampaging cows in this field,' she said when she could speak. When they finally made it back to the hotel the other guests viewed them with interest, but were too polite to ask why they were covered in mud from head to foot.

'There seems to be a lot of mud in our lives,' said Simon, recalling their run to the Pennyrest Hotel.

*

He returned to his office on Monday morning refreshed and energised. His first inspiration was to ask Piers to take up the subject of Andecis' independence with Adam Falls. I've been relying too heavily on my own resources, thought Simon. That's a sure sign of stress and lower-self behaviour. I'll spread the load and relax about the end result.

When the time came to tell the rest of the company about the deal, Simon made an impassioned speech to his board. The UK members were sitting in the boardroom in Mayfair, and the European directors were on the video conference screen. There was a three-line whip; everyone was present.

'Tomorrow is going to be an important day for us. We're holding a press conference with Tantron Pine, and announcing to the world our intentions to merge. I don't want the employees of Andecis to hear of this for the first time through the media or gossip. The last year or so has shown us how successful we can be when we pull together as a team. You are helping me, Piers and the others to negotiate a good deal for all of us, which preserves what makes us successful. This spirit of collaboration is our strength. Now I want you to get on your bikes and use any method appropriate to get this news to your teams personally before nine am Eastern Standard Time tomorrow. Then please use the way we have handled it on the board as a model for communicating with and reassuring your teams.'

The next six months were hectic. Simon remembered the effort they had all put in to buying Delster and Zeus, but this was double the work. He was caught up in the merger activities: due diligence, people due diligence by Tantron Pine of the Andecis top team, and interminable meetings with the key players in the pharmaceutical giant. Negotiations continued to be tough, especially with Enrico, but Simon kept his mission in his sights, and remained calm and confident. He let go of the outcome, knowing it would happen if meant, and all in good time. He put a lot of effort into keeping his troops informed of developments, and encouraged Piers and Tony Albertino to do the same. Yet at the same time he had responsibilities for continuing to run the company, and for many of the tasks which Piers had delegated following his illness.

Carolyn continued to be an invaluable ally to Simon during

this time. She shared Simon's dreams and his faith in the mission. She often helped him to get back into his higher self when the going got tough. David Jones, promoted now to UK head of research, was also a staunch supporter. He did everything he could to communicate with, and encourage the research teams to develop a positive attitude towards the merger. The uncertainty inherent in the deal created an inevitable response of alarm and negativity from many people, but he did much to keep this to a reasonable level.

Simon and Carolyn saw even less of each other than before. They continued to spend weekends together, but often he had to pore over documents all day Saturday and much of Sunday.

'It's only your love and understanding that keep me going,' he said to her.

'Not so. I'm gratified that it helps, but it's your faith in the mission that's really doing the trick.'

'You're right as usual,' said Simon, quite happy for this to be the case.

Holidays were put on hold, apart from Christmas spent with Carolyn, Edward and Katy in Mauritius. Katy was now at Oxford and struggling, but hanging on. Edward was still at school, and passing his exams, even though all his reports said 'Could do better'.

After Christmas things seemed to quieten down, and Simon began to wonder if the merger had hit a hitch. Then in February he was suddenly called to a meeting with Adam Falls at the Tantron Pine head office in Chicago. Simon had never been to Chicago before, and was surprised at the beauty of the city. He and Piers were put up in the company apartment just around the corner from the imposing head offices. Adam took Piers and Simon to lunch in a private dining room on the thirtieth floor of the office building with views over Lake Michigan, and the lakeshore of the city. It was a fine sight. They were glad to be viewing the lake from a heated building as it was minus twenty degrees centigrade outside. Simon could see the waves crashing on to the shore in the wind. He did not know what the chill factor was, and didn't want to find out.

'I don't know whether you've said anything to Simon?' Adam started with a question to Piers, who shook his head.

'I thought it would be best coming from you.'

Simon wondered what on earth that remark presaged.

'Simon, Piers is stepping down as chief executive of Andecis. He will see the merger through, but suggests that you take over as head of Andecis when you're part of Tantron Pine.'

Simon looked at Piers in surprise; he had not seen this coming. He knew his job in the new merged company would be secure, as was his mission to continue producing drugs for older people, but he had not realised how well he was regarded.

Adam continued, 'We plan to keep Andecis as a separate, independent company for a time, and we want you to run it as global head. We're very impressed by the culture you've created in the company, particularly in the European part. We see it as part of the reason for your considerable success. We also think that you're leading the field with your IT solutions. I want you as the new head of Andecis to help us to share in your achievements. You will of course have a place on the board of Tantron Pine.'

'Wow!' said Simon, and immediately offered up a silent prayer of thanks. He realised that during the quiet spell Piers had probably been working away with Adam to achieve independence for Andecis in the merger. Letting go of the outcome had been the right thing to do.

'I take it that means yes?' asked Adam. Simon, of course, agreed. It all felt very right. The offer was not yet spelt out in detail, but it suggested to him that his own board would remain intact. He would need the support of his team to take the mission forward after the merger, and it looked now as if he would have it. His only worry concerned Piers. He wasn't sure if he was going voluntarily or was being pushed out, which Simon did not think he deserved.

That evening Piers explained his position to Simon over dinner at the apartment. They were sitting with their feet up on the coffee table, having just eaten a takeaway Thai meal, and were about to tuck into some ice cream. They were both very relaxed.

'It's nice to leave pomp and ceremony aside for a while,' Simon said as he finished his Diet Coke.

'I'm sorry to have left you in the dark over this decision of mine. It was a very sudden one. In fact I only made up my mind finally last week,' Piers told him.

'That's OK, Piers, I know you like to play your cards close to your chest, and you have every right to do so over such a personal decision as this.'

'I've been re-examining my whole life since the heart attack, as you know. At first I thought I wanted to carry on at Andecis, but latterly I've found that my heart is just not in it. Metaphorically, I mean. I want to have a life before I die, which hopefully won't be for a long time if I look after myself. I'll keep on a few non-executive chairman roles, do some charity work with my wife, and spend time with her in nice parts of the world contemplating my navel.'

Simon kept his counsel, but he knew that the last part of Piers's plan would never work. 'I'll miss you, Piers, you've been instrumental in any success I've had in Andecis,' he said as they parted the next day.

Piers stayed around giving strong support to Simon until the completion of the merger. Later that year, when Andecis became part of Tantron Pine, he disappeared, and they all lost touch with him. Simon was even busier after the merger, and so was Carolyn. They saw less of each other than ever before, but the relationship continued to be a joy and a strength to him.

Simon had tried to persuade his mother to let him buy her a house in Holland Park, near to him, so that he could keep an eye on her as she grew older. He went to visit her in Scotland to put this proposition to her, sitting with her in the parlour of her tiny house in Kirkconnell Lea. The fire was blazing in the hearth, and they drank strong, hot cups of tea. It was a warm Indian summer day in September and he was sweating in the tiny, closed up room. His mother lit the fire in the parlour whenever she had visitors, winter or summer. It would have been inhospitable for her to fail to do so.

'I would rather stay up here in Scotland with real people than end my life with people who have only money and glamour to offer the world,' she said grimly.

Simon sighed and did not raise the subject again. He realised he couldn't win. At least I have the children and Carolyn in my life, he comforted himself. Driven out by the heat in the small room, he left soon afterwards. 'I love you, you eccentric old bat,' he said as he gave his mother a goodbye hug.

Simon felt very supported by Carolyn, his team at Andecis

and his children, but his real strength came from within, from his new interpretation of commitment. He had cultivated the habit of listening to his inner voice and following its guidance. Underlying this commitment was his trust in the playing out of his destiny. He had learnt that whatever he needed at any stage of his journey to meet his destiny would be made available to him, a sharp contrast to his old belief in the need to seize fate by the throat and do whatever it took to succeed, against all odds.

He was now in a state of wondering surrender and he noticed that when he was in that state he exerted an enormous allure, not to women (he had all he wanted in Carolyn), but to people and events that would take him forward. Without thinking himself special, he nevertheless noticed that people were attracted to an authentic presence and to the unfolding of a future that seemed full of possibilities. He felt as if his life was a series of miracles.

Later that year on New Year's Eve he opened his dressing-table drawer, looking for cuff links for his dress shirt. He and Carolyn were going to a black-tie party given by friends around the corner from her house in South Kensington. They were both spending the night at her house, so they could walk home after the party. While searching for his cuff links he found the engagement ring he had bought and not yet given to Carolyn.

Something made me hold off from giving that to her, he thought to himself. It wasn't just the merger excitement and uncertainty over the future, I think I may have sensed that it was premature before. With luck the time is now ripe. I'll take it with me and give it to her on New Year's Day. That's a symbolic day for me anyway, a day on which my life has seen some significant changes in the past. We're at a wonderful stage in our lives. We've worked far too hard for the last two years or so, but the merger is now a reality, and Andecis continues to do well. My shares in the company are worth so much that I don't need to continue working, and yet I'm highly motivated to keep moving the mission forward. Things should begin to settle down in the company this year, in fact, very soon. We'll be able to start leading normal lives again.

As Simon dressed for the party at Carolyn's house that night, he chatted to her about the first time they'd heard Angela talk at the Institute of Directors.

'She has helped the two of us to change our lives an incredible amount,' said Carolyn, 'as has Red Roger.'

Simon laughed. 'I probably learnt more from Red Roger, but that's not to say I haven't learnt a lot from Angela.'

'Do you remember how she started the talk?' asked Carolyn. 'Just how many of those attributes of peace do you think you have in your life now? None of us in the audience that day could claim to have even half of them.'

'Yes, I do. Let's see. I do have my fair share of inner peace and harmony, and I experience spontaneous humour and delight, especially with you around,' he said, giving her a kiss and helping her as she struggled into a tight evening dress that covered most of her delightful body, but not all.

'I'm not so sure if you're unhurried and free from busyness. That'll have to be a goal for both of us for the New Year,' said Carolyn.

'I'll drink to that,' said Simon. 'I don't struggle and feel fear so much any more, and when I do lapse I have you and Angela to put me gently back on course.'

'Glad to be of service. I remember her telling us that transformation is a journey you shouldn't try to make on your own.'

'I'm full of energy and enthusiasm, probably because I don't descend into my lower self so often any more. And I certainly have loving friendships and intimate relationships,' he said, kissing the tops of her breasts where they peeped out from the tight bodice of her dress.

'You get eight out of ten, Simon Bruce,' said Carolyn, stroking his cheek and straightening his bow tie.

'Don't make me big-headed. Angela keeps saying that just when you think you've cracked it, the universe gives you yet another lesson to learn. She said that to me for the first time just before we were kidnapped.'

'Get those fear images out of your head and take me to the party.'

They strolled along the Old Brompton Road to the party in the Little Boltons. It was a mild damp December evening, but they were happy, and didn't mind the dullness. Just before they arrived the sky exploded into a riotous display of fireworks, and the winter night was lit up. They stood for a while watching, hugging each other for warmth, and when it was over rang the doorbell of their friends' house.

The party was terrific. They stayed so late that their hosts served them breakfast before they left.

The doorbell woke them at about noon the next day. Carolyn put on her robe and went downstairs. Simon decided to follow. He was awake now, and was looking forward to a pleasant, if slightly hungover, New Year's Day, with a world full of opportunity awaiting him. He wondered why that dreadful sense of foreboding was nevertheless gnawing at the pit of his stomach, but he put it down to too much champagne the night before and went to see who was at the front door.

When he got downstairs he heard voices in the drawing room so he went in to join them. The visitor was Piers! He and Carolyn were standing together in the middle of the room. Carolyn had turned to stone. Her green eyes were wide with wonder; her mouth was slightly open. Piers had a bouquet of yellow roses in one hand, and a ring with the biggest diamond Simon had ever seen in the other.

'Oh, I didn't realise you'd be here, Simon,' said Piers, as ever oozing confidence and mastery of the situation. 'Actually, that's no bad thing. It's best you hear this from the horse's mouth. My wife and I have parted, and I've come to ask Carolyn to marry me.'

You can get in touch with the author at:

The Change Partnership
Ryder Court
14 Ryder Street
London SW1Y 6QB

Tel: 020 7451 0452